SHADOWS

Maggie Berke, grandest of the Hollywood grand dames, retired from acting to support her son, a talented child film star. But cruel fate, in the form of pneumonia, soon ended his career. Blaming herself for his demise, Maggie remains in her Hollywood mansion with her stepdaughter. But there are dark shadows in her life, and a growing sense of fear that leads her to invite her niece, Mari, to visit her. Mari soon begins to suspect that the old woman is terrified of something . . . and to share her fear.

V. J. BANIS

◆

SHADOWS

Complete and Unabridged

LINFORD
Leicester

First published in Great Britain in 1970

First Linford Edition
published 2015

A catalogue record for this book is available
from the British Library.

ISBN 978–1–4448–2410–0

Published by
F. A. Thorpe (Publishing)
Anstey, Leicestershire

Set by Words & Graphics Ltd.
Anstey, Leicestershire
Printed and bound in Great Britain by
T. J. International Ltd., Padstow, Cornwall

This book is printed on acid-free paper

1

I did not know of the ghosts when I first saw Movie Manor. The house ruled a hillside over the Sunset Strip. I thought it looked aggressively bleak, with an abundance of gray stone that made it seem oddly affected.

Of course, Maggie Berke did not call her house Movie Manor. To her, and to thousands and thousands of old movie fans, it was The Aerie, lofty in name as well as perch. It was my mother, Maggie's sister, who had given it that less respectful name. And not that she didn't respect Maggie's position in life; she just did not take it very seriously.

'You'll find Maggie a very sweet person,' she told me shortly before I left Minneapolis. 'I must confess, I always was rather bored with all that movie talk and Hollywood gossip and such. That's why I haven't tried visiting Maggie in all these years. But I expect you'll find it exciting, at least at first; and unless things have changed a great deal, Maggie ought to be able to give you some help with your career.

'And don't tell her I call her house Movie Manor,' she said. 'It would deflate her terribly. She calls it Eagle's Roost or something of that sort.'

Movie Manor, The Aerie, Eagle's Roost — whatever one chose to call it, it was impressive, if not warming. It sat in sprawling stony splendor and cast stained-glass eyes on the serfs that toiled on the street below. The drive seemed to wind about the hillside forever, and all the while there was the house popping in and out of view, your gaze unable to escape it. If you looked away, the drive twisted, and the house was once again in your line of vision.

I had been here before, twenty years ago. But I had been only four then, so I remembered nothing at all about the place, and very little about my aunt — except that she would not tolerate being called Aunt Maggie, and that she had been incredibly lovely, even in mourning. She had lost a son at that time, and the whole world shared her loss.

Buddy Berke was every mother's son, everyone's little brother, every child's playmate. He had been the cutest, most talented, most famous of the child stars, just as his mother before him had been the grandest of the screen's grand dames.

She had retired voluntarily ('I want to quit while I'm on top.' How often had that remark been quoted?), setting her career aside and devoting herself exclusively to his. Fate, in the form of pneumonia, had subsequently and soon ended his.

However, she said in her letter that she still had 'connections,' and of course I was flattered that she wanted to help my career along. I was here also because I was curious about the legendary Maggie Berke. She may have been my aunt, but I knew no more about her than any other movie fan.

'You'll be very disappointed,' my mother insisted, 'to learn that she's exactly like what they say in those movie magazines — very grand, very elegant, always 'on camera'.'

Still, I wanted to see for myself.

The cab reached the entryway at last. The man helped me bring my bags up to the door and I tipped him generously. Then I lingered, nervous at having arrived. I smiled at the cabbie as he started up and drove down the drive. Finally I lifted the big brass knocker, a grim dragon's head, and brought it down with a sharp crack. There was a long pause and then, creaking appropriately, the door opened on a wizened little creature.

'I'm Mari Andrews, Miss Berke's niece,' I said, although her query had been in her eyes only. 'Miss Berke is expecting me.'

'She'll be down shortly,' the woman said, ushering me into a vast entry hall. 'Wait here.' With that she was gone, shuffling away and leaving me quite alone.

I could not help staring about. It was a splendid place, with a domed ceiling towering four stories above me, one of the towers that gave the façade such an imposing look. A massive chandelier gleamed overhead. The floors were black and white marble, the carpeting on the stairs a crimson red, and everywhere was gilt and crystal in awesome excess.

'Mari.' She did not say it like 'Mary,' which it was to my family and friends, but with a broad a, so that it sounded foreign and exotic. I turned to find her smiling.

She paused on the landing of the great stairs and opened her arms in a gesture of welcome. I knew instinctively how the scene was to be played. I was to rush across the foyer and up the broad stairs, all the while aware that my carriage and grace were being measured, while she stood serenely poised, waiting to embrace me.

Had I thought of it in advance, I would have expected it to be just like this, and I didn't mind, really. I was prepared to treat Maggie as the great star that she was.

What I was not prepared for was Maggie herself. I remembered her only vaguely, but those vague impressions were of a breathtaking beauty. In the years since I had seen her I had seen countless photos of her, in magazines ranging from *Movie World* to *Life*. Of course she had aged over the years, and the photos had reflected this; they had shown a woman maturing gradually and gracefully, but scarcely less beautiful for all the march of time. In this instance, however, the cameras had lied.

The truth was, she was a little old woman. Even at a distance I could tell that. I would not have recognized her in a million years, except for that familiar pose — hip thrust to one side, arms outstretched, head thrown back in a frozen toss of laughter.

For a woman who sought to be an actress, I acted very badly. My surprise was blatantly, if fleetingly, evident. I recovered myself a second later, but that time had been long enough to do the damage, and I saw her chin droop slightly.

It had fortunately been long enough also to save my life. Had I dashed straight for her, as I otherwise would have done, I would have been directly under the chandelier when it fell. As it was, I had only taken a step forward when there was a shriek of tearing metal. Someone had appeared on the stairs just beyond

Maggie, and she screamed in chorus with the metal. Maggie's hand went to her breast and her eyes went upward.

I say all of this as though it happened slowly — indeed, there was a sense of slow-motion about the scene — but in fact it could not have involved more than a second or so.

Afterward, Maggie said she had enjoyed my self-control. I looked, it seemed, quite cool and self-possessed. 'Nerves of steel,' she was to say. 'A born actress.'

In fact, I was so bewildered that I only half comprehended what was happening. The stranger on the stairs ran down to the landing and threw her arms protectively about Maggie.

'I told you!' she screamed, staring wide-eyed at me although it was clearly Maggie she was addressing. 'I told you there'd be trouble if she came here.'

'Shut up, Elisa,' Maggie snapped. She shrugged off the protective embrace and, forgetting her script, came down the stairs swiftly. 'Mari, are you all right?'

'Yes, I think so,' I said, looking from Elisa, to Maggie, to the debris on the floor. Had I been a few steps further across the room, I would be part of that debris now, and surely dead!

'You're crazy if you stay!' Elisa shouted from the stairs, looking as terrified as I was suddenly feeling. 'I tell you that was only the beginning.'

★   ★   ★

It was a spectacular welcome to The Aerie. When I got to know Maggie better, I concluded that it was almost the sort of thing she herself would have staged for effect — except that it wasn't the right effect. No matter what she said about my poise, I was shaken. So was she. When she came anxiously around the debris to clasp my hand in hers, I saw that she was terrified. Her calm was all a sham; her hands trembled and her eyes glittered with fear.

I said the first silly thing that came into my head: 'You certainly do things in a bang-up manner here.'

She laughed, but she sounded on the verge of hysteria. 'Good girl,' she said, squeezing my hand. 'Keep up the show. You never know who might be watching from the wings.'

Elisa had followed Maggie down the stairs and now stood glowering at the broken chandelier. The ruckus brought back the frail little thing who had admitted me to the house. Close on her heels came a man. He looked straight at the heap of broken glass and metal and then shot me a glance. I don't know why but I shivered under that scrutiny. I felt as though those hard, cruel eyes had, in one look, stripped my body and soul bare. Had it not been for that look and the cruelty apparent in his face, he might have been good-looking. As it was, he made my skin crawl.

'What's wrong?' he demanded sharply — not, I thought, in the tone of voice a servant would use; I had thought him that.

'The light fell,' Elisa snapped back at him, frantically twisting her hands together in front of her flat bosom.

'No one hurt?' They both looked at me.

'I'm all right,' I said, forcing my voice to sound quite natural. I did not want him to see that I was afraid of him. I felt instinctively that in some way he would manage to use that knowledge to his own advantage.

'It's only pure luck that she is, though,' Maggie said. 'She could very easily have been killed. How did this happen, anyhow?'

'Chains broke, I expect,' he said rudely, staring down at it and poking at one twisted piece of metal with his shoe. 'I told you a week ago I thought it needed replacing.'

'Did you?' For a fleeting moment Maggie looked confused. Then she took hold of herself again, and said, 'Yes, of course. I forgot.' She turned back to me. 'Then it's my own fault; I'm entirely to blame. I hope you'll forgive me, dear.'

'Of course.'

'Davis, get rid of this mess, for Heaven's sake. And Elisa, I hope you've gotten over your screaming long enough to meet your cousin.'

Elisa came sullenly over to where we stood and gave my hand a tepid shake. I had not placed her until then; indeed, I had quite forgotten all about her. Elisa

10

was one of those poor creatures who are so easily forgotten. She was a pale and colorless thing, about my height, and with a lumpy figure in which all of the lumps were misplaced. She had obviously spent some money on her coiffure, and her dress was not inexpensive, but the hair seemed not to suit her and the dress was so colorless as to make her still more nondescript.

My first instinct was to pity her, but the hatred she let show in her eyes when she came to meet me stifled that emotion. I was shocked by it.

'Forgive my loss of decorum,' she said with just the faintest edge of sarcasm in her voice. 'Some of us tend to show our real feelings too easily.'

If Maggie noticed the sarcasm she gave no sign. 'I expect you're tired from your trip. Come into the solarium and have something to drink. Then I'll let you go up and rest.'

'Something cold would be nice,' I said, following her into a big bright room decorated in prints and rattan and artificial palms.

'Yes, iced tea, I think. Elisa, go tell Miss Wright we'd like some iced tea.'

I glanced at Elisa in time to see her sullen expression. I did not think she was in the habit of having her stepmother tell her what to do. I saw her hesitate, but her better judgment prevailed and she went quietly off in the direction of the kitchen.

'Well,' Maggie said when we were alone. 'Let me look at you.' She stepped back to give me a frank appraisal.

I smiled and pirouetted at her request. I was not, I knew, truly beautiful, but neither was I so silly as to think myself homely. I had very long and very black hair, although it was pinned back sedately just now. I had a well molded face and clear pale skin. I was a little too slender, but I knew that photographed advantageously.

She nodded approvingly. 'Yes, you've got the Berke looks all right. Not as good-looking as I was at your age, but better than your mother.' She winked and added quickly, 'Don't quote me on that. I'll deny it if I see it in print.'

'Mother sends her love, and regrets

that she couldn't make it this trip.'

Maggie threw her head back and laughed. 'It would take wild horses to drag her out here,' she said. 'She hates Hollywood. She always said it was all fake. It is, of course, but I love it. And you will too, I can tell. I saw it in your eyes at the very first glance.'

'Well, if my feelings are so transparent I'm not going very far as an actress,' I said.

She dismissed that suggestion with a wave of her hand. 'It isn't acting that makes you a star here. I've watched scores of fine actresses come and go without making more than a little ripple. No, it's flair; it's that inner magic, and nobody can teach it to you either. You either have it or you don't. I had it. Nobody ever stopped to question whether I could act or not.'

'Well, I don't know if I have that or not.'

She gave me a shrewd look. 'I don't know either. Maybe . . . just maybe . . . '

Elisa came in, with Miss Wright at her heels, bearing a tray. Maggie supervised,

13

and I had my chance to study her. She had never been tall, but she had always managed to carry herself as though she were. Now her shoulders were bent as though under a heavy load. Her body had been voluptuously perfect, her skin luminescent.

Of course, there had to have been some changes. Maggie was nearly sixty now. But she was thin to a point of being gaunt and her skin was like fine writing paper, stretched taut. Her glorious auburn hair was completely white; I wondered when she had stopped dying it.

However, in her face there lingered the ghost of her former beauty. It hadn't been only physical beauty; it had been . . . well, that flair she spoke of, I would say. And she still had that. In repose, when she thought you weren't looking, it was just an ordinary, aging face. But when she was 'on camera' — when her features were sparkling and animated — you could still see the Maggie Berke who had received, at the height of her career and even afterward, scores of marriage proposals with every mail delivery.

'There,' Maggie said when we were all served and seated, Maggie occupying a chair twice as tall as she was and, not by accident, I suspected, rather throne-like. 'Now tell me about things at home. Your mother still makes dresses, I suppose?'

I couldn't be really annoyed by the deprecating way she said it. No doubt to Maggie Berke, Gala Originals fell under the heading of making dresses. We were not in the category with Galanos and the designers she was accustomed to, but the line had been highly successful none-theless, and had recently begun to attract attention in Chicago and New York.

'She's doing very well at it,' I said aloud.

'Oh, she was always quite good,' Maggie admitted. 'Although not for me. I thought once I'd have her do some things, but there wasn't a single one of the designs she sent that I could possibly have worn. They were all for mature women.'

The designs had been sent only five years ago. I think my mother had made them deliberately 'mature', to give her sister a hint, or a dig. She hadn't seemed surprised when they had been returned with a polite 'no, thank you' note.

'Mari's come out to be an actress,' Maggie informed Elisa, giving us both a look as though she knew things we did not.

'So I've heard,' Elisa said with no show of enthusiasm. 'I wish you luck, of course. It's a hard business, as Maggie's no doubt already told you.'

'I'm only giving myself a year,' I said, unable to help resenting Elisa's patronizing tone. 'That's long enough to find out if I have what it takes to make a go of it. If not, Mother's trained me in the business, and I always have that to go back to.'

'She sings and dances,' Maggie said, again to Elisa, but in almost an aside. 'Although God knows, that never made any difference out here. She has a pretty figure, though. Do you think it's as good as mine was?'

One corner of Elisa's mouth tilted slightly upward. 'That's not likely,' she said. Then, fixing her cool gray eyes on me, she said, 'No offense, but Maggie's figure was considered the most perfect in the world.' She said it not as though she believed it to be true, but as though she were repeating an often-stated line from a script. I had realized immediately that Elisa did not like me and did not want me there. Now, I suddenly realized she did not like Maggie either.

'I always felt such a lame duck,' I said, 'with all the talented people on this side of the family. You, and Buddy . . . '

Maggie's glass slipped from her fingers and crashed to the floor, sending tea, ice, and slivers of glass in all directions.

'Maggie, I'm sorry.' I seemed to be doing a great job of bringing things down with a crash. Of course Buddy had been her son, and of course he had died tragically. But that had been twenty years before, and I had never dreamed that mentioning his name would have startled her so.

Miss Wright chose this particular moment to come to the door and say, 'The doctor is here, Madam.'

'Oh blast!' Maggie's famous composure was nearly as shattered as her glass. 'Elisa, I thought I told you to cancel today's appointment.'

'I'm afraid it must have slipped my mind,' Elisa said, busy sponging iced tea off her skirt. 'Miss Wright, have the doctor wait in the library, please, and then come back and look after this mess.'

Elisa's head was down, so Maggie did not see the quick smile that flitted across her features. At first I did not understand it, and thought perhaps that I had only imagined it, but then it became clear to me. Maggie had not wanted me to think her an invalid, subject to regular visits by her doctor. Elisa had deliberately forgotten to cancel the appointment purely to embarrass Maggie — I was certain of that.

'It's all right,' I said, standing. 'I'm really a little tired. Perhaps I'll take a nap after I've unpacked.'

'I'm having some people in for dinner tonight,' Maggie said. 'I'm afraid it may be a little stuffy. None of the guests are young anymore, but they're a few people I thought you ought to meet. Sam Carr will be here; he's still rather good as an agent. And there'll be a producer or two here as well. It's at seven. A black dress will do fine.'

'Thank you. And . . . Maggie, it's good to be here.'

'It's good to have you here, isn't it, Elisa?'

'Very,' Elisa said. Her eyes said something more along the lines of, 'It would be good to have your head on a platter.'

I gave her my most dazzling smile and left. However, the difficulty in making a dramatic exit is that it is so awkward to have to go back for anything. Not until I was in the hall and started for the stairs did I think of the one detail we had all overlooked. I did not know where my room was.

The entryway was empty. The chandelier and its broken glass were gone, leaving as the only evidence of what had happened a few cracked tiles on the floor and, overhead, a string of dangling wires. My luggage was gone, presumably to my room.

I turned and started back to the solarium, but I stopped just outside the door to that room. Maggie and Elisa were arguing, their voices slightly raised. It was not difficult to tell that I was the object of their conversation.

'She shouldn't have come here,' Elisa

was saying. 'I told you he wouldn't like it, not a bit.'

'That's preposterous. Why should he care?' Maggie argued. But her voice was not the instrument of command I had heard a short time before. It was pleading, almost whining. 'Besides, I'm frightened. I wanted her here.'

'Mark my words,' Elisa said. 'They'll find her dead one morning.'

2

I suppressed a gasp of disbelief. They could only be speaking of me, but the remarks made no sense at all. Who was the 'he' who would disapprove of my coming? And why should he? And did Elisa really think I was in danger? I thought of the chandelier. Surely that had been an accident, hadn't it?

I realized suddenly that they were crossing the room, and that I was eavesdropping. I turned and went quickly across the foyer, toward the first open door that I saw. I didn't get through it. Instead, I collided with the man coming out of that room.

'Hey,' he said, putting an arm around me to catch me.

'Well, Doctor Wolfe,' Maggie said behind me. 'I see you've met my niece already.'

He let go of me and I blushed at Maggie's mocking smile. 'Not formally,' he said, grinning at my embarrassment. 'Hello, I'm Doctor Kenneth Wolfe, who's trying to be the man in your aunt's life.'

'I'm Mari Andrews,' I told him. 'And I suspect you'll only be one of many.'

His look told me he was only joking; that his interest in Maggie was professional. It also hinted at some interest in me, not quite professional. And I was thinking if this tall, handsome Viking didn't arouse my aunt's famous romantic instinct, she really had gotten old. Doctor Kenneth Wolfe ought to have been a screen actor himself. He had the sort of striking good looks that made women's hearts beat faster. Mine certainly was.

'Well, Doctor,' Maggie said, interrupting the looks we were giving one another. 'If you haven't completely changed your plans, perhaps we can get on with the business.'

'Where you are involved, dear woman, my business is my pleasure. I hope I'll see you again, Miss Andrews.' He cocked an eyebrow, making a question out of it.

'She's going to be here for a year,' Maggie said with a sigh. 'And as you're in and out of this place almost daily, I suspect you'll run into one another.' She paused and then added thoughtfully, 'As a matter of fact, why don't you come for dinner tonight, Doctor. I'm having some people in but there isn't a person within decades of Mari's age. You might at least speak her language.'

He scowled. 'Tonight? That's rather short notice.'

'It's not necessary,' I said, embarrassed. But he gave me a look, so I said, 'Of course, if you could make it, it would be nice.'

'I'll make it,' he said, giving me a wide grin. 'It'll give me a chance to see if this she-devil is following my advice.'

'I can tell you right now,' Maggie said, 'that tonight I won't be. I have no intention of letting dinner guests see me drinking warm milk. It'll be champagne and caviar, and it's just as well you will be on hand, if worse comes to worst.'

She swept past him, into what presumably was the library. He gave me another smile that did horrendous things to my pulse, and followed her, closing the door softly. Elisa and I were left in the hall.

'I'm afraid,' I said, addressing her in as friendly a manner as I could achieve, 'that I don't know which room is mine. Can you show me?'

'Second floor, third door on the right,' she said coolly, and left me alone, returning to the solarium.

★　★　★

I had no difficulty finding my room, of course, but my cheeks were still smarting when I entered that pastel-colored chamber. If I had had any doubts at all regarding Elisa's feelings for me, that final rebuff would have ended them. Not only did she dislike me intensely, but she did not even mean to pretend otherwise when we were alone.

That's fine, I thought, giving my suitcase a poke with one foot. I set myself to unpacking, taking my anger out on my clothes.

By the time I had finished putting everything away, I had calmed down. It was not my nature to return tit for tat.

Elisa had insulted me, but I knew enough about human nature to know that this sort of behavior was usually a defense mechanism to hide unhappiness or insecurity.

I went to sit by the window, where I had a spectacular view of the Sunset Strip. It was mid-afternoon, but already the street was thick with swift traffic. Pedestrians strolled singly or in groups, and the pedestrians on this particular street were as often as not very colorful sights themselves. There were girls with long hair and boys with longer hair. Many of the males sported beards and mustaches and long sideburns. The clothes were brilliantly colorful; I watched a boy in lipstick-red pants and vest to match. In Minneapolis he would have provoked a great deal of staring; here he only seemed to fit in naturally.

Of course Elisa was unhappy. How could she help it? It could only be unpleasant to be the ugly duckling in a family that included both Maggie and Buddy Berke. Even Elisa's father, I had been told, had been a handsome creature.

Maggie had been his second wife. I knew nothing about the first, but I could conjecture that Elisa must have inherited her plain looks from her. There was poor Elisa surrounded by lovely, witty charmers competing with one another for center stage, a center stage she could never hope to occupy.

What had her life been like here? I had only the vaguest memory of her from that other visit, so little of an impression had she made. Hadn't her father and Maggie been divorced? It seemed that I recalled they had. If so, why was Elisa still here?

Anyway, I thought with a smile, I had much more pleasant things to think of. I was in Los Angeles, embarking upon what might be a new career. I was in Aunt Maggie's lovely house, I had a glamorous evening before me, and I had just met a terribly exciting man, whom I would see again in a few hours. So I truly had no reason to remain surly.

I looked around my room. When I first came in, I had scarcely noticed it. It was pleasant enough; expensively furnished, but a little too fluffy for my tastes.

Probably Maggie had decorated it herself. It had her quality of overstatement that could be either exciting or exasperating.

Strangely enough, although the room had a tendency toward fussiness, the walls were for the most part bare. There were candelabra on either side of a lavish mirror, and a small shelf with figurines. The only other wall ornament was a huge portrait of Buddy that dominated one entire wall. The eyes that stared down at me were familiar, not only because they were so much like Maggie's, but because Buddy himself remained familiar twenty years after his death. His movies were seen regularly on television. Bookstores displayed his face on posters, and no book or program on movies could be complete without some discussion of Buddy Berke. The young boy with the tousled hair and the extra-large eyes had come very close to doing what no one else in films had been able to do — eclipse his famous mother.

Indeed, in this house it seemed as if he had succeeded in that. It occurred to me that I had seen another of Buddy's portraits in the hall, and there had been a picture of him on the stairs. One would have expected Maggie, with her glamorous past and her lingering vanity, to make this house a shrine to herself. If anything, however, it was like a shrine to her dead son. That thought struck me as odd.

On the dressers were some photographs in little gold frames. I went to look at them. They too were of Buddy, in various movie roles. Here he was in the diminutive sailor uniform of *The Little Captain*, and next to it, the street urchin of *Little Boy Blue*.

I've never credited myself with precognition, but just then, for a moment, I had a sense of uneasiness, a quick shiver of fear that is described as someone walking on one's grave. I looked around, and I would not have been surprised to find that I was no longer alone, that someone was staring at me. However, the room was still empty, and the only eyes on me were those of Buddy Berke. I did not know then how significant that fact was.

I threw open one of the windows. It was January. The air was crisp and cool, with none of that smog for which Los Angeles is famous. It would be impossible to remain gloomy for long in the face of that buoyant sunshine, so glorious after the crystalline winter of Minneapolis. Even the incident with the chandelier made me smile as I recalled it. What an exciting story that would make when I wrote to Mother.

I freshened up a bit and set out to have a look around the house and grounds. The afternoon sunshine lured me outside first. The grounds were impressive. There was a pool that looked as big as some of the lakes back home, and a tennis court that looked like it hadn't seen much use lately. There were carefully tended flowers blooming everywhere in profusion, making one forget that Los Angeles was by nature a desert, which people had spent years turning into an oasis.

I could not resist the temptation, natural to anyone who has lived all her winters in snow and ice, to stoop and test the water of the pool. It was warm, and I promised myself a swim at the first opportunity.

'Not today, though,' I said to myself. The fact was, it had turned suddenly very cool. I did not know then how quickly the January temperature drops in the late afternoon in southern California.

There was a pool house next door and, finding the door unlocked, I went in. Inside, I found Maggie's personal shrine. Here there were no pictures of Buddy, only of herself. I stood studying the life-sized portrait on one wall. Yes, she truly had been beautiful, with a beauty that transcended the mere physical. I thought back to all the movie magazine stories. How old had Maggie been when she retired from the screen? Forty, at the most. Not so old by movie queen standards and, certainly, she had still been ravishing. Had she quit because she sincerely wanted to put Buddy's career first, or was it because she could not bear the inevitable — seeing her own aging process in the eyes of her beholders? Had it been a noble gesture, or a shrewd one designed to make a legend of herself?

There were other pictures of her here. I looked at numerous photos of Maggie and found a scrapbook on one table devoted to press coverage. She had been, even by Hollywood standards, big news. Some of it, of course, was the work of press agents. But her two Oscars were real. So were her three marriages; Elisa's father had been the fourth and last.

I was so absorbed in that glamorous but shadowy figure from the past that I did not know I had been joined by the flesh-and-blood Maggie until she spoke.

'Beautiful, wasn't she?' her light silvery voice said behind me. I whirled about, startled by the unexpected sound.

Maggie laughed and pointed at the scrapbook. I had been staring at a photograph taken during the filming of her last movie. Maggie had been exquisite, at the very peak of her loveliness.

'Yes, she was,' I said, smiling back at her. 'And is,' I added quickly.

'Tush.' Maggie made a clicking sound with her tongue. 'Do you think I've lost my eyesight as well as my looks? No, I made a career of illusions, but I never had any about myself, and I don't have any now. That Maggie Berke who thrilled thousands of men the world over is gone. She died years ago.'

It would have been silliness to dispute what she said. In fact, I was glad to know she could look at life so frankly.

Maggie came to stand beside me. She took the scrapbook from my hand and stared hard at the same photograph I had been studying.

'Beautiful,' she said, closing the book softly. 'They all said I had never been more beautiful than in that film. I can't tell you the parts I was offered after this one. I could have played any role I wanted, at almost any price I cared to name.' There was a dreamy expression on her face as she relived that heady past.

'Yet you gave it up, like the snap of a finger,' I said.

She gave me a quick look. 'And you're wondering why,' she said, with a mischievous grin.

I grinned back. 'Yes, frankly. I've read so much, so many different theories.'

'Theories,' she snorted derisively. 'Hogwash. None of them knew. They were just guessing. They still do.' She fixed those brilliant eyes on me, and they were electrifying; you could never look away from those eyes once they had seized you in their grip. 'Oh, I admit, I wanted the legend status. You get that by quitting at the top, as only a few smart, very brave ones can do. Garbo did it, and it worked for her. But of course, she wasn't as big as I. Ponselle did it in opera, and everyone remembers her as better than she was. But I really was *good*. I knew how I would haunt them as the years went by.'

She put the scrapbook back on the table, in exactly the same spot where I had found it, in exactly the same position. I realized how many times she must have returned it to that spot after studying its contents.

'But it wasn't that,' she said. 'No, I retired for the very reason I gave. To devote myself to my son's career.'

'It was a very noble thing to do,' I said, feeling some remark was required of me.

She laughed aloud. 'Oh ho, that's the rib, because it does sound noble, doesn't it? And all those people who knew me, especially the gossip mongers, could only say exactly the same thing. It galled them because they all knew I wasn't noble, not Maggie Berke. What they never saw was that it wasn't noble at all. That's been my little joke all these years.'

She fixed her gaze on me again, and she looked of a sudden feverish. 'The screen was my life, don't you see. It was like life blood to me. But I was too smart not to see that for me it was almost over. I was nearly forty. No amount of magic or makeup could have given me more than ten years, unless I wanted the character roles, and I wouldn't have them. I'd never give them a chance to laugh or shake their heads in phony sympathy, not on my behalf. I had a friend who was working night and day on television. He told me it would replace movies before my decade was ended. He said I'd go out with a fizzle because there would be new people on television. It would require new young stars.'

She had become increasingly agitated. Her hands brushed nervously at the air about her, as though to shoo away hovering ghosts. 'So I made a decision. I decided to make a star of Buddy. I knew he had talent. He'd already had a modest success in *The Tin Soldier*, and I knew with my know-how I could make him really big, bigger than any of the others. Temple, Rooney, Bartholomew, Garland — they were like so many wind-up toys compared to Buddy. I promised myself to make him as big as I had been. He was a mere tot. Don't you see? I could share his career. He would be the new talent television wanted. Through him I could go on and on.'

She paused, clutching at her throat. I tried to think of something to say to calm her. I had begun to fear what this agitation might mean for her.

'I still think it was very great of you to give up your career for his,' I said. 'You didn't have to stop just then. You could still have made movies. I think your television friend was overly pessimistic. In retrospect, you had at least ten years ahead of you.'

'I didn't give it up,' she said, her voice rising. 'That's the trouble, don't you see? If I had, Buddy would be still alive today, and he'd be the star he was destined to be. But I couldn't give up the spotlight.'

'But I thought you stopped filming after . . . ?'

She was wild-eyed as she interrupted me. 'Oh, I stopped filming, of course. But I couldn't give up the rest, all the trappings of being a star. I couldn't give up the parties, the adulation, the life of glamor. And I killed Buddy because of it.'

She threw her hands over her face and began to cry. For a moment I stood helpless, staring at the frantic creature she had become. What did she mean, she had killed her son? I had an ominous vision of the portrait in my room, the portrait of Buddy. Those larger-than-life eyes stared down as though mocking, as though they held a secret known to them alone.

Even as I reached out to comfort Maggie, I could not help asking myself: was this their secret?

'Maggie,' I began.

But as quickly as this excited state had come it was gone. Maggie passed a hand over her eyes and when she again looked at me, she was calm and fully in control of herself. It was uncanny to see how she cloaked her emotions so that you did not know what was real and what was only play-acting. I began to perceive how she could have fascinated the world of her generation. But I could also see how difficult it could be to come really close to Maggie; to the real Maggie — whoever that was.

'You must think I'm a crazy old woman,' she said with a laugh. 'It's just that, with so little present, and almost no future, the past becomes so vivid to me. I don't expect you'll understand that, not for another forty years or so. But take my word for it, it will make sense to you some day.'

She shivered and clasped her arms about herself. 'It's getting cool. That's one of the oddities of California living, in case no one has warned you yet. No matter how warm and pleasant a winter day may seem, the nights are going to be cool. And speaking of nights, we have a full one ahead of us, and an important one. I want you to look your very best at dinner tonight, my dear. Shall we be going in?' She let me hold her arm and we went back into the main house. At the stairs we parted; I to go to my room, Maggie to consult with Miss Wright regarding the evening meal.

It had gotten late. By the time I had bathed, dressed my hair, and made up, it was time to dress for the evening. I took out my best dress — not one of our own designs, but a name label — and slipped it on. It was black and classically simple. I had chosen it because it made me look older. With the required pearls, and my hair sedately up, I looked closer to thirty than twenty-four, and almost slinky. Almost, but not quite.

The pearls went back into their case, and the slinky black number into the closet. I let my hair down, the way I wore it at home, and brushed it mercilessly until it fell in a glowing cascade about my face and over my shoulder. Finally I took from the closet one of the Gala Originals I had brought along. I had designed this one myself, for myself, and I had been waiting for the right occasion to wear it.

If ever there was going to be a right

occasion, I thought, this is it. The dress could not have been redder if I had been dressed in flames. It was filmy and wispy and little-girlish, and floated about me when I walked like a crimson cloud. I wore no jewelry with it; it would have been superfluous.

When I came down a few minutes late, the sound of voices from the library told me the guests were gathered there. For only a moment I hesitated outside the door. Was I being too stagey? Would Maggie disapprove? After all, she had suggested a simple black dress.

I smiled to myself. If there was anyone likely to appreciate independence, it was Maggie. With that, I walked into the room, puffs of red trailing me.

It was a successful entrance. Everyone in the room turned, and in that first moment it was easy enough to read every reaction. There were three men I didn't know who looked pleased to see me. There was a man I recognized from photographs as Sam Carr, one of Hollywood's most illustrious agents and of course Maggie's agent; his eyes widened appreciatively. As for

Maggie herself, although she suppressed the smile that sprang to her lips, I had the impression she was quite pleased. The only disapproving response was a sullen look from Elisa, who had exchanged her previous dress for another, equally beige.

The reaction that pleased me most, however — and for which, I realized afterward, I had immediately looked — was that of the young, handsome doctor I had met earlier. My eyes sought Ken Wolfe. He was there, and at the sight of me he whistled softly. I was pleased.

Of course all of this lasted only a second or so. Maggie swept across the room to me, eyes twinkling, and Sam Carr was close on her heels.

'Who taught you how to make an entrance like that?' he asked jovially.

'You forget she's my niece,' Maggie said proudly, putting an arm about my waist. 'Mari, this is Sam Carr — positively the most reprehensible man I know, but a passable agent if you keep a close eye on him.'

'I hope she does keep an eye on me,' Sam said, bowing.

I was introduced to the three strangers, all older men, whose names slipped quickly in and out of my mind. One was a director and the other two were producers. At any other time I might have been impressed. For the moment, however, my thoughts were dominated by Ken Wolfe. He was quick to move to my side when Maggie left it to get me a cocktail.

'I hope you aren't forgetting which of us you come here to see,' she said when she came back, bringing me a cold and crystal-clear martini.

'Some men are capable of more than one love,' he said, toasting her with his drink. She laughed, but even though she knew his flirtation with her meant nothing, she was clearly pleased by the flattery. I did not know whether Ken Wolfe was any good as a doctor, but he certainly understood a woman's vanity.

We chatted pleasantly over drinks. One of the producers, a man named Best, asked about my experience and my ambitions.

'As to the experience,' I said, 'I really haven't much. I've done a few little theater things, but that's all. And my ambition? Well, I think I want to be an actress, but only if I'm good enough to really make it successfully. That's why I'm here . . . to find out.' That earned me a peculiar look, but Maggie chose that particular moment to change the subject, and I didn't learn what it was my interrogator had been thinking.

At dinner I found myself seated across from Ken, and between Elisa and Sam Carr. I liked the agent. He had a florid manner and appearance that suggested grossness, but in fact he was charming and witty, a delightful companion. However, I was aware the whole time of Ken's eyes watching me with appreciation.

'Your aunt didn't tell me what a pleasant young thing we were going to be meeting,' Sam said over coffee. 'I'd have been altogether eager to get here tonight if she had.'

'I should think with Maggie and Elisa here you'd have been eager anyway,' I said. I had tried throughout the meal to engage Elisa in our conversation, but with a spectacular lack of success.

'Yes,' Maggie said from the head of the table. 'That wasn't very flattering, Sam. Elisa, we shall have to make him suffer in some way, shan't we?'

Elisa looked from one to the other of them, and for a fleeting instant her eyes flickered across me. Again I had a shocking realization of how intensely she disliked me.

'Sam's head is easily turned,' she said sourly, and returned her attention to her coffee.

'Frankly,' Ken said, 'your niece would turn any man's head.'

I blushed slightly at the profusion of compliments, and Elisa's scowl deepened, but Maggie laughed. Although she pretended to be jealous, she seemed to be basking in the attention being showered on me.

'I can see that if Elisa and I are to get the slightest attention from anyone here,' she said, 'we're going to have to eliminate the competition. Doctor Wolfe, why don't you show Mari how lovely our California nights are?'

'Love to,' he said, jumping up with

undisguised enthusiasm.

'It isn't necessary,' I said, although I was as eager as he was.

'Nonsense,' Maggie said imperiously. 'It certainly is. We want to talk about you, and that's so awkward if you're here. Go along now. Elisa, would you like to join them?'

I saw Ken's face fall at this suggestion, and I admit it took some of the edge off. I remembered my promise to try to overcome Elisa's dislike of me, however, and I said quickly, 'Yes, Elisa, why don't you come with us?'

She fixed her gray eyes on me; they coldly gave the lie to her smile. 'Thank you, but I think not. If everyone will excuse me, I think I'll go to my room. I have some sewing I want to get done.'

Maggie tossed her head. 'Sewing. For Heaven's sake, why don't you let Miss Wright do that?'

'Because I like sewing,' Elisa said, standing. 'It's *my* talent.' She walked heavily past Ken and me, and left the room.

44

3

The view from the terrace was utterly breathtaking by night. Close below us was the Strip, a carnival of lights and color and bustling throngs. Although it was only an ordinary night in January, there was a holiday atmosphere about the street. You expected a parade to come by any minute; indeed, the denizens of the street were a parade in themselves. Some of them even played upon musical instruments. All that was lacking were the elephants. There were clowns, and uniforms, and dancers and musicians and singers, and strolling players. Beyond all of this thrilling confusion lay the city of lights, sprawling as far as the eye could see. A blanket of jewels; I had heard that cliché so often. But it did look like that — shimmering, twinkling, incredibly colorful and incredibly lovely.

An impetuous breeze sent my dress billowing. I shivered slightly, and Ken's arm came around my shoulders. 'Cold?' he asked.

I looked up at him and smiled into his handsome face. 'Not now,' I said.

For a few minutes we talked little. Ken pointed out a few of the landmarks. 'Your first visit?' he asked.

'I was here as a little girl, but I don't remember much. Somehow I never expected it to be this beautiful.'

'It can be,' he said. 'Or, it can be unbelievably ugly. Why don't you let me show you around a little? The office is closed tomorrow.'

'I'd like that,' I said, and felt the pressure increase slightly about my shoulders.

We came around the house. The pool, lighted at night, looked like a vast aquamarine set in a green setting. Ken led the way to a bench nearby and we sat down.

'Doctor,' I began.

'Ken,' he corrected me.

'Ken,' I said, smiling at him. 'Is Maggie's health all right? You seem to be paying rather close attention to her — or do you give all your patients such service?'

He chuckled softly. 'No, but then you have to admit, your aunt isn't like other people.' After a moment he added, more soberly: 'Actually, I'm new with your aunt. The doctor she had before retired recently due to his own health. I bought his practice. I've only been treating your aunt a few weeks. Frankly, I'm not sure there's anything at all wrong with her physically. I have a notion Doctor Walker may just have been catering to her need for attention, but I've run quite a few tests the last couple of weeks and I should know pretty quickly where we stand.'

Something in his inflection made me ask: 'You said there might be nothing wrong with her physically. Were you implying perhaps she might have some other kind of difficulty?'

He was silent for a moment before he said: 'Again, I don't know. Don't get me wrong; I'm not implying Maggie Berke is off her rocker or anything like that. But she is a highly emotional type. Most actresses are. And unstable. There is something . . . I don't know what. Something that I can't quite put my finger on.'

'Yes, I understand,' I said thoughtfully. 'I had the same feeling. Maggie acts like someone who's haunted. And Elisa . . . '

He laughed again. 'She doesn't seem to have taken to you,' he said.

I nodded ruefully. 'No. I get the impression that she would as soon see me dead as speak to me.'

'You're pretty rigorous competition for an old plow horse like Elisa.' I started to object, but he lifted a hand. 'No, it isn't just a matter of physical beauty, although you have that in abundance. There are countless women no prettier physically than Elisa, who still manage to be attractive and charming. Elisa's problem is what's inside all that plain flesh. In there she really is an ugly woman.'

I turned my head to look at the big old house, lifting upward toward the dark sky. 'I suppose she's lived an unhappy life,' I said.

'Yes.' He was silent for a moment. 'How much do you know about . . . about the things that have happened here?'

'Not very much, I'm afraid. As I said, I was a child when I was here last, and although my mother and Aunt Maggie are sisters, Mother never talked much about Maggie's private life.'

'I looked into it when I first learned Maggie Berke was going to be my patient. A great deal of it came from Doctor Walker. He's known Maggie since she was a big star. The rest I picked up here and there.'

I suddenly remembered something that happened earlier. 'Maggie said something today, something I didn't understand. She said she had killed Buddy.'

He smiled, but it was a sad expression. 'Yes, in a sense she might have. At least, that's how she sees it. That's a big part of her problem: the guilt she still suffers over that.'

I waited silently for him to explain, knowing instinctively that he would do so in good time; that he wanted to talk to me about it.

'I guess you know the part about Maggie retiring — giving up her career so she could manage her son's?' I nodded. 'Well, of course, 'retiring' for Maggie meant that she wasn't making any more films. I'm not going to try to go into her motives; enough people have discussed them already. At any rate, I'm only interested in facts. What I do know is that although she wasn't filming, Maggie remained very much the queen of Hollywood. She was still a star — The Star, as I hear it. No party was a party unless Maggie was there. Whatever she said or did was copied from one end of the city to the other. If she was seen at a certain nightclub or restaurant, it immediately became *the* place to be seen.'

'And her son?' I asked when he paused.

He shook his head. 'Most people would like to think he suffered as a result. But the apparent truth is, he didn't. Maggie doted on him; she idolized him. Oh, he was often in the care of a babysitter, but bear in mind, this was a late-night town in those days. By the time Maggie went out, entrusting Buddy to a nurse, he was long since in bed asleep. He probably wasn't even half aware of her social life, unless he noticed that she slept late in the mornings.

'If anybody was neglected, it was Elisa.

When her father was killed in an accident, which was after he and Maggie were divorced, he left nothing. Elisa was a penniless orphan. Of course, Maggie took her in. Basically Maggie's a very generous person. And there were probably subtler psychological factors. Haven't you ever noticed how the really beautiful creatures, the birds-of-paradise, frequently attach themselves to someone rather dumpy-looking? It makes the lovely one look even lovelier.'

He paused again for a moment. 'Anyway,' he said finally, 'whatever her motives, she took Elisa in. I suppose at first Elisa was grateful. Probably later, when she'd had time to think about it, she was resentful. To be not only the ugly duckling, but financially dependent as well, must have been a bitter pill to swallow.

'But she stayed — nothing else to do, presumably. She took care of the house, and took care of Buddy. She came to be the regularly assigned nurse.

'As you know, Buddy took sick. It didn't seem to be much more than a bad cold. Maggie was expected to attend a big premiere, and it was up in the air all day whether or not she would go. In the end Elisa, who for once had been invited too, said that she would stay with Buddy, so that Maggie could go. Maggie went.'

This time the pause was so long that I did prompt him to continue. 'Go on,' I said softly.

'Buddy took a sudden turn for the worse,' he said. 'His fever shot sky-high. It would be all too easy to blame Elisa. She should have called Doctor Walker, or simply taken Buddy to a hospital. Instead, she tried to take care of him herself, and to find Maggie. But Maggie had gone from the premiere to a big party — that's the usual thing — and Elisa didn't find her.

'By the time Maggie returned home, nearly dawn, it was too late. She called an ambulance at once, but the child died before the ambulance even arrived. According to Elisa and Maggie, he cried for his mother. Elisa said the entire night he had screamed and pleaded for Maggie, unable to understand where she was.'

We were silent for a long time. 'And so

Maggie blames herself for not being here,' I said finally.

'Yes,' he said. 'And although she never mentions it, I suspect Elisa blames herself too. And the two of them became near recluses in this house. I was frankly glad to hear you were coming, even without knowing how pretty you would turn out to be. Maggie rarely entertains, although I think it might be the best medicine in the world for her. She needs anything that will bring her back to life again, and help her over this morbid obsession with her son.'

'And it's haunted her for twenty years now,' I said. I looked again at the house. Somehow it seemed less friendly now, as though a pall of gloom had settled over it while we talked. 'Twenty years haunted by the shadows of the past. I never knew.'

He switched suddenly to a more cheerful tone of voice. 'Well, your coming seems to have brightened up the place already. Maybe you're the medicine she's needed all this time.'

'I hope so,' I said, letting him help me to my feet. But even as I said this, I was wondering — would I truly be able to help Maggie? Or would I, like she and Elisa, succumb to the tragic ghosts that haunted this place?

★   ★   ★

'We were hoping you hadn't eloped,' Maggie said as we came in; she accompanied the remark with a mischievous grin.

'I tried,' Ken replied. 'But she insists on a church wedding.'

'Then I've still got time to get my bid in,' Sam Carr said. My cheeks turned faintly pink, although of course I enjoyed the flattery.

'Brandy?' Maggie asked, indicating the tray and glasses before her.

'Thanks,' Ken said, 'but I've got to head for home. Early call tomorrow.' He turned to me, taking my hand warmly in his. 'I have to go by the hospital in the morning, but I can be free shortly before lunch. Still want to do some sightseeing?'

'I'd love it,' I assured him. I didn't need any acting ability to sound interested.

When he had gone, I became aware of

a waiting atmosphere. For the first time I remembered that Maggie had asked Ken to take me outside so that she could discuss me with her business friends. I looked around; all of them were watching me — waiting, presumably, for the right time to speak.

'Well,' I said, looking from one to the other, 'what's it to be? A career as an actress, or back to dress-designing in Minneapolis?'

From the silence that fell, I guessed at once what the consensus would be. Sam Carr attempted to soften the blow. 'If that thing you're wearing is any indication of your design talents,' he said softly, 'you'd be foolish not to exercise them.'

While acting had not been a burning ambition with me, I could not help but feel chagrined. 'I've been told I act well,' I said meekly.

'I suspect you probably do,' Maggie said. 'No doubt far better than I ever did.'

'And we've all agreed,' one of the producers said, 'that so far as physical beauty, you're up there with the best of them.'

I looked at Maggie. She, as well as the others, was being kindly and sympathetic, but unyieldingly frank. 'That flair you spoke of earlier?' I asked.

She smiled and shrugged. 'Too early to tell about that, actually. You might have it, if it were brought out.'

The initial disappointment had passed quickly. I felt much calmer than I would have expected to feel, but I was at a loss to understand how they had reached what was obviously a unanimous decision.

'Then what . . . ?' I said, and stopped.

The producer named Best came to my rescue. 'The difficulty is that you don't want to be an actress.'

'But of course I do,' I said, surprised at the reply. 'That's why I'm here, in California, to see whether I can make it or not.'

He smiled indulgently. 'Ah, that's the point right there . . . to see whether you can make it or not. A real actress, you see, would be here to make it, no matter what.'

'It's another of those plus factors,' Sam Carr added. 'An instinct, almost. A

56

determination. You'd vaguely like to be an actress. It would be pleasant, but it isn't an obsession with you, a compulsion. And for the great ones, the ones who matter, it must be. When you were asked before, you said you think you want to be an actress. That's not nearly enough.'

'Do understand, dear?' Maggie said. 'If you just want to play around at movie-making, we can arrange to get you a few parts. You can no doubt train yourself to be a very competent professional.'

I sat beside her on the sofa, not looking at any of them. I understood exactly what she was saying, and although it was blunt to the point of being cruel, it was quite right. I had come here only with a tepid desire. I could not even pretend to be heartbroken at their criticism. It had been only a lark, and they had recognized at once my lack of sincere motivation.

I looked up to find them all watching me anxiously, no doubt afraid they had been too harsh. I gave them a smile, and saw each of them in turn relax. 'No, you're right,' I said. 'I'm a designer, and a good one, and it would be foolish to give up a career in which I will excel for one in which I'll never be more than mediocre.'

'Although a very pretty mediocrity,' Sam Carr said quickly.

'Hear, hear,' Maggie agreed. She put an affectionate hand on my shoulder. 'I hope you don't regret coming, however. I want you to stay as long as you like.'

I thought of Ken Wolfe. 'No,' I said aloud, 'I don't regret coming to California. And thank you, all of you, for your honest appraisal. I think it's probably saved me a great deal of wasted time and effort, and probably a much greater disappointment later.'

The guests left a short time later. Sam Carr in particular insisted that he would see more of me in the next few days. When they had gone, Maggie took my hand in hers and accompanied me up the stairs.

'You will stay for a few days, won't you?' she asked, pausing outside my door.

'I'd like to, yes,' I said. 'After all, this is my first grown-up visit to California, and there's so much I'd like to see before I go home.'

Maggie smiled. 'And you have such a handsome guide to show you around.' I blushed and would have protested, but she gave my hand a pat. 'My dear, you've nothing to apologize to me for. By your age I was married to my second husband. And neither of them was as handsome as Doctor Wolfe.' With that she was gone, and I fled to the privacy of my room.

Once I was in bed, however, I found that I was still too keyed up to sleep. I lay for a moment staring at the ceiling. Then, with an impatient sigh, I slipped from the bed and moved quietly across the dark room to the window. Although it was late the city still looked busy.

A movement closer below caught my eye. I pressed my cheek against the glass to see the terrace. A gray figure separated itself from the darker shadows. As she moved silently and quickly across the terrace, I recognized Elisa. In a moment she was gone, disappearing into the darkness beyond.

She had come and gone so quickly I almost thought I had imagined seeing her there. But no, the sight had been real. She had long ago retired to her room. Why, then, should she be stealing about like this in the dark of the night?

Of course, Elisa had every right to go in and out and around the house as she chose. No doubt she had countless reasons for wanting to cross the terrace at nearly midnight.

I went to bed, still certain that I would not sleep. I must have fallen asleep at once.

I woke with a start, sitting up in bed. The room seemed strangely too dark, and I realized dimly that the outside lights, which had before sent a faint glow into the room, were now out.

It was a moment before I identified the sound that had awakened me: the click of a lock. I sat in the darkness staring at my door as though it might explain itself. When it did not, I threw back the bedclothes and stood. It had gotten quite cold in the room, and I took a minute to fetch my robe from the closet and slip it on. Then I stole to the door that opened onto the hall.

It was locked. I ran my hand over the

lock-plate. Yes, it was the old fashioned sort; nothing so modern as throw-locks in this old house. It was the sort of lock that required a key to turn it. On my side, the lock was empty; that must mean that the key was on the other side, the hall side.

And that meant that someone had locked me into my room!

Once again I had the sensation of someone walking over my grave. A convulsive shudder ran through my body. For a moment I stood in frozen silence, and in that interim I heard, or thought I heard, the sound of breathing on the other side of the door.

'Hello,' I said aloud, rattling the knob. 'Is someone out there?'

For an answer, a floorboard creaked. Again the sense of panic rose up in me, and I rattled the knob harder. 'Who's out there?' I demanded, more loudly. 'Who locked this door?'

Silence.

'Let me out!' I fairly screamed this. I was past caring whether I disturbed the others in the house. I began to pound on the door, yelling, 'Open this door! Let me out!'

The door opened so suddenly that I was nearly knocked to the floor as it swung inward. Maggie and I stared at one another in mutual confusion.

'Mari,' she said, looking beyond me to see that I was alone. 'What on earth's the matter? I heard you yelling and pounding and thought the Russians had invaded.'

'I was locked in my room,' I said, breathing heavily. Now that the door was open and I was no longer alone, I suddenly felt a little foolish. But the lingering ghost of my fear was real.

'But that's impossible,' she said. 'I just opened the door myself without a key. Look.' She turned the knob in her hand. There was no key in the lock; I could see that at a glance.

The door across the hall had opened and Elisa came out, wearing a cotton robe. She gave us a curious look.

'But it was locked,' I cried. My eyes went to Elisa. 'Why didn't you come sooner?' I demanded angrily. 'Surely you must have heard me yelling and pounding?'

She gave me the sort of glance one gives a rowdy child. 'I take very strong pills to help me sleep,' she said calmly. 'It's difficult for me to wake once I've gone to sleep, until they've worn off.'

'That's true,' Maggie said. Her voice sounded unsteady, and when I looked back at her, I saw at once that she was greatly distressed. She was staring with unblinking eyes at the lock on the door, but I could tell that she saw much more than just the metal. Whatever it was that filled her inner vision, it was quite horrible. She swayed, and I thought she was going to faint.

Elisa moved with astonishing speed for one of her bulk. Before I had recovered from the shock of Maggie's distress, Elisa had crossed the hall and taken her stepmother in her arms. Maggie turned stricken eyes upon her. I had a feeling that some dreadful understanding passed between them, some message guarded from my comprehension.

I was still frightened, angry, and confused. 'I don't know what to say,' I stammered. 'It was locked. I know it was.'

'Perhaps you were having a bad dream,' Elisa suggested coolly.

'Yes,' Maggie said. 'It must have been that, my dear.'

I made no reply. I was aware of Maggie's unhappy state, and I didn't want to make it worse by arguing with her.

'Come along,' Elisa said to Maggie, supporting the older woman. 'Let me take you back to your room.'

'Yes,' Maggie said faintly.

Elisa paused to look back over her shoulder. 'Perhaps you'd like one of my pills. I never dream when I take them.'

'No,' I said firmly. 'That won't be necessary.'

I closed the door upon them, but once I was out of view from those cold eyes, I leaned weakly against the wood and pressed my hands to my temples.

A bad dream? Surely not. But if not, then who had locked me in my room, and why? Elisa might have locked the door and, when I began pounding hysterically instead of rattling the knob, she might have slipped across the hall to remove the key before Maggie came to investigate.

As for her assertion that she hadn't heard me, that her sleeping pill was too strong, that was nothing but nonsense. I had seen her outside earlier, far from asleep.

But why had she lied about any of it? What possible motive could Elisa — or anyone, for that matter — have had in locking my door for a moment or two?

4

By morning the incident seemed just that — an incident. But I could not entirely dismiss what had happened. It was a mystery that lingered at the edge of my consciousness while I bathed and dressed, and was still there when I came down to breakfast.

Maggie was at the table when I came into the breakfast room. Seeing her again, and seeing how pale and drawn she looked, I was conscious that in some way and for some reason the incident had disturbed her more than it had me. Even her greeting was vague and preoccupied.

'Hello, dear,' she said, turning her cheek for me to kiss. 'Miss Wright will be here in a moment to see what you'll have, and the coffee's right there, still plenty hot.'

'Thank you.' I poured myself a cup of the strong-looking coffee and sat down. In a moment, Elisa had joined us. If

Maggie and I had slept poorly, Elisa looked altogether refreshed and rested. Nothing had disturbed her sleep.

'I hope you had no more bad dreams,' she greeted me, helping herself to coffee.

'I slept like a log,' I lied. I thought she sounded altogether too pleased with the idea that my sleep had been disturbed. I was quickly abandoning the idea of ever being friends with Elisa.

I had scarcely finished eating when Ken Wolfe called. 'All set to see the sights?' he asked.

'Straining at the bit,' I told him.

He laughed and the sound dispelled my lingering gloom. 'I'll be there in twenty minutes,' he said.

Impatient to be outside and away from the atmosphere of gloom that I sensed in the house, I was waiting at the steps when Ken pulled up in a gleaming white sports car, its top down — a Triumph, I learned later. He leaned across to open the door for me and I slid quickly into the low-slung front seat beside him.

It was a perfect day for sightseeing. The California sun was bright and warm.

This, and Ken's infectious good spirits, soon had me in a better mood. I had intended to tell him about the mysterious happening during the night, but instead I forgot all about it. We drove and talked of a myriad of things, ranging from my dress designs to Ken's early struggles to rise from poverty through education.

'I thought you were a California native,' I said when he mentioned his Montana childhood.

'I'm afraid they're rare creatures,' he replied. 'Everyone you meet here, or almost everyone, is from someplace else. Usually someplace where it's cold and snowy.'

Of course we couldn't begin to see the entire city in one day, although we seemed to cover a great many miles. I got my first real look at the Pacific, in Santa Monica, and strolled along a colorful pier where a magnificently antiquated carousel was in noisy operation.

From there we drove what seemed to be across the state, but was only to downtown Los Angeles, where I saw the Civic Center, the elegant Music Center and the

Disney Hall. Lunch was in a little Mexican shop near the original plaza of the town, followed by a stroll through a neighborhood that might have been lifted straight from Tokyo. Before the afternoon was done I had seen a homey Jewish neighborhood that out-New Yorked old New York, as well as Russian and Greek Settlements, a tiny Bavarian shopping area, and Chinatown. I was astonished at the city's many faces.

'And you haven't even got a glimpse of Hollywood,' Ken said, amused by my childish delight. 'Or the studios. Or Disneyland, or Malibu. This was just my dollar-twenty-five special. Wait until I really show you around.'

We arrived at the observatory in vast Griffith Park just in time for a special show that took us, almost too realistically for comfort, to the moon and back. It was late afternoon when Ken led me to the high balconies behind the observatory building.

'One of my favorite views,' he said as we stepped to the wall.

It was breathtaking. The city stretched

for mile upon mile. I thought surely we must be seeing all of it, but he assured me otherwise.

'All of the valley side is behind the mountains,' he explained. 'Vast, isn't it?'

'And lovely,' I said.

'So are you,' he said softly.

I knew as soon as I looked up at him that he was going to kiss me.

Suddenly we became aware of some youthful giggling and turned to find that we had an audience of amused youngsters.

Laughing, we waved to the youngsters and went back to Ken's car. It was twilight by the time we arrived back at the house.

'You've got exactly an hour to dress for dinner,' Ken said, kissing me before I got out of the car. 'Pick you up then.'

'I'll be ready,' I promised. At the door I turned back to watch him drive away. I felt I was the luckiest girl in the world.

I went to look for Maggie, to tell her I would be out for the evening. I found no trace of her in the downstairs rooms, but Miss Wright, busy in the kitchen, said she thought Maggie was on the terrace.

I did not find Maggie, but I did witness an unpleasant incident. As I came around the corner of the house, I saw a stray dog sniffing around the terrace. He was only a mongrel, but quite harmless-looking. I did not see anyone until a stone was thrown at the dog, hitting him on his flanks and sending him racing away, yelping with pain.

I looked in the direction from which the stone had come in time to see Davis, the hired man, about to throw another one.

'Stop that!' I shouted.

He paused to give me a disdainful look. In that length of time, however, the animal had managed to escape. He threw the rock futilely in that general direction. With another look at me, he turned away.

'My aunt will hear of this,' I said to his back. If he even heard me, he gave no indication of it, but went on his way, disappearing behind the garages.

I found Maggie and Elisa in the sunroom, and angrily told Maggie what I thought of Davis. I fully expected her to be as angry as I was. To my surprise, however, it was Elisa who answered my charges.

'Davis is responsible for keeping the grounds up,' she said with no show of concern. 'Under the circumstances he can hardly be expected to encourage every stray dog in town to come hanging around.'

'He need not resort to cruelty, either,' I retorted. I turned to Maggie for support.

'Perhaps we're making a mountain out of a molehill,' she said. 'It was, after all, just a stray, wasn't it? I suppose the poor creature is quite accustomed to that kind of treatment.'

I was surprised by Maggie's attitude, but more than that, I was puzzled. Perhaps I was only imagining it, but I thought I saw a quick exchange of glances that passed between Maggie and Elisa, and for whatever reason, Maggie decided in that split second to accept Elisa's verdict as her own. It was disappointing and frustrating, but this was Maggie's house, and Davis was her employee.

'Perhaps you're right,' I said. I could

not miss the expression of triumph Elisa wore.

★   ★   ★

High over the city in a rooftop restaurant, I told Ken of the incident at dinner. I was pleased to see that Davis's behavior angered him.

'Too bad I wasn't around,' he said, scowling. 'I'd have taught him a thing or two about cruelty.'

'What puzzles me,' I said, 'is that Maggie should countenance it. I've never thought of her as a cruel person.'

'Nor have I,' he admitted. He was thoughtful for a moment. 'Still,' he went on, 'there's something peculiar about that household. As a maintenance man, Davis is inadequate at best. Take a closer look at the grounds tomorrow. They aren't kept up the way they should be with a full-time man around. I've often wondered why Maggie keeps him on when she could get someone better qualified.'

I thought about what he had said. On reflection, it was true that the grounds could and should have looked better with Davis there full time, even living on the estate. I thought about the accident when I arrived; the falling chandelier. Oughtn't that to have been taken care of before the accident had happened?

'Maybe Maggie can't fire him?' I suggested tentatively. 'Maybe he has some sort of hold over her, some lever to assure him his place there.'

He smiled and reached across the table to pat my hand. 'Maybe, but frankly that sounds a little too cloak-and-daggerish for me. Granted Davis is a bad egg, but Maggie's getting older, and she tends to be a little lazy. Maybe in her mind he does an adequate job. For all we know, maybe she only pays him a minimum wage.'

Just then the waiter arrived with our salads and the conversation was changed. 'After all,' Ken said, a romantic gleam in his eye, 'I have far more important things on my mind.'

'Such as?' I asked.

'Such as coaxing a very pretty young lady to fall in love with me,' he said.

5

I had come to The Aerie with a sense of joy and excitement, and although I had been here only a very short time, in their place was a sense of foreboding. I was uncomfortable in the house without comprehending why. I felt myself surrounded by shadows; phantoms that dissolved quickly enough when the light of reason was turned upon them, but returned as quickly when darkness came. I thought of ghosts, in a literary sense; the ghosts of Maggie's haunted past. I did not know then how appropriate that thought was, nor that Maggie's present, and The Aerie, were still very much haunted.

Another peculiar incident occurred a few nights after my dinner with Ken.

I left my room late that night. Unable to sleep, I meant to get myself a drink of water from the kitchen. It was a moonlit night, and I did not need to turn on lights to find my way, although I descended cautiously. Halfway down, the wide stairs curved, almost doubling back on themselves.

It was when I had just rounded the bend in the stairs, moving slowly and quietly, that a movement below brought me to a stop. A figure in white moved soundlessly across the hall, disappearing into the library. I stood frozen. The impression that I had seen a ghost quickened my heartbeat, and for the first time I was aware of the fear that had been growing in me.

My reaction had been instinctive. What I had seen was someone real — Maggie, or perhaps Elisa. In the darkness I couldn't distinguish who it was, but logic told me it was one or the other.

I was proven right. I had just started down again when Maggie came from the library, passing for a moment through a patch of moonlight so that I had a clear look at her. I paused, meaning to call to her, but something restrained me. She had not seen me. Indeed, the expression on her face was so intense, so concentrated, I doubted whether she would have seen me even had she chanced to look in my direction, which she did not. She moved as noiselessly and quickly back across the hall and went into the sunroom. It seemed as though she were searching for something.

It's none of my business, I told myself. *She has every right to wander about her own home in the night, and to do so undisturbed.* I turned to ascend the stairs, deciding after all that I did not need a drink of water. I had just again come round the bend in the stairs, when Maggie said from behind me, 'There you are. You did come! I knew you would. I told her you would.'

I looked back, over the bannister. Maggie had come to the bottom of the stairs. Her upturned face brimming with excitement, she caught up her nightdress in her hands and began to run up the stairs toward me. Standing where I was, I was partially hidden by the stairs, and in shadow, so she did not see me clearly.

'Maggie . . . ' I said, puzzled by the strangeness of her behavior.

At the sound of my voice she stopped still. In a moment she had realized who I was. I could actually watch the excitement drain from her face, to be replaced by disappointment. The strength fled her frail shoulders and they slumped noticeably.

'Mari,' she said. 'What are you doing here? Why aren't you in bed?'

'I came down for some water,' I said. 'Maggie, is anything wrong?'

'Wrong?' She wore a dazed look and shook her head wearily. 'No, nothing's wrong. I often ramble around late at night. It's part of growing old.'

'Would you like me to keep you company?' I asked.

'No, no that won't be necessary. I . . . ' Her voice broke suddenly, and she began to cry. She threw her hands over her face and her body shook with her sobs.

'Maggie,' I cried, starting toward her.

'No,' she said again, shaking her head firmly. 'It's nothing. It will pass. Leave me alone, please.' She turned and fled down the stairs, leaving me to stare dumbfounded after her. She disappeared into the library again. I stood listening to the faint sobs.

Finally, although it broke my heart to leave her like that, I made my way back to my room. The sound of her crying lingered in my mind, as did that first excitement when she had seen me on the stairs.

'There you are . . . You did come . . . ' What had she meant? Clearly she had mistaken me for someone else. But who? Elisa? The thought that some other person, someone perhaps a stranger to me, might have been wandering those halls with me sent a shiver along my spine. Why had she been so disappointed to discover me? Why had she begun to cry? 'I told her you would . . . ' She had cried that also. Whom had she told?

The same questions continued to hover in my mind, even after I had fallen asleep, so that I woke feeling more exhausted than when I had gone to bed, and no more knowledgeable.

At breakfast, Maggie made no mention of our nocturnal meeting, and taking my cue from her I avoided mentioning it as well. The thought crossed my mind that perhaps Maggie had been sleepwalking. I made a mental note to ask Ken about it when I saw him later.

'I thought if you were free today,' she said, seeming bright and completely rested, 'that perhaps you'd like to come with me to the studio, and let me show you around. It will be so much nicer than those dreadful tours. You know, notwithstanding all the years, they still treat me like a queen.'

'But you are,' I said. 'The reigning monarch of the movie world.'

She grunted, although I could always tell that she was pleased by flattery. 'But at any rate, you'll get to see the real works, if you're interested.'

'I'd love it,' I said, and meant it sincerely. I had been looking forward to seeing the inside of a studio, and secretly hoping that perhaps Maggie could accompany me on such a tour. I would never have asked her directly, however, for I did not know what memories such a visit might bring to her mind.

'Do you drive?' she asked. When I nodded, she said, 'Good. I'll be ready in half an hour.'

Of course, she was not ready in half an hour. But when she joined me some forty-five minutes later, it was as a woman I had not before seen face to face. Despite her age, she looked every inch the glamorous movie star. Her dress was exquisitely flamboyant, and she wore a cape trimmed in leopard. She wore a golden wig, and makeup had worked considerable magic on her face. But it was her figure that made her look young and lovely: she was still slim, and she still carried herself with the confidence of beauty.

'Davis brought the car around for us,' she explained, offering me her arm as we went out.

The car, which she identified as a Daimler, was a mammoth, elegant machine that might have been older than I was. I had never driven anything quite so grand, and for the first few blocks, swept along in the Los Angeles traffic, driving took all my attention.

Maggie seemed not to notice. She gazed from the car window at the passing sights. People stared, of course, and a few even recognized her, or at least waved as though they did.

She waved back grandly. I noticed that she sat carefully back in the seat, and away from the glass, so that they had only a faint image of her. I could not help wondering how often she had driven this route, waving to veritable throngs of fans.

I remembered that once a young man had thrown himself in front of her car because she had not answered his letter in which he had proposed marriage. He had not been killed, but he was injured. Maggie paid for his hospital bills, and although he did not get to marry her, he did enjoy her company every day of his convalescence.

It was only one of many such incidents in her glamorous past. Did she miss them now? I wondered. Again I thought of the night before. Of her giddy excitement, her disappointment, and the lonely sobbing that followed.

I was so absorbed in driving the car and in my own reflections that I was startled when Maggie spoke, breaking the silence.

'I'm afraid I haven't been altogether

honest with you,' she said. 'I've been meaning to make a confession to you. I suppose there's no time like the present.'

'I hope it's nothing too drastic,' I said with a small laugh.

She smiled across the car seat. 'No, it's only that I took advantage of you in inviting you here. You see, I said I wanted to help you with your career, but it wasn't that at all.'

'I don't understand,' I said.

'I knew before you ever came what the verdict regarding your career would be. Just from the letters you wrote me about it, I could have told you everything that we said to you after dinner the other night. So you see, I encouraged you falsely, for my own selfish motives.'

'Well, since I wanted to come to California, it's hardly worth an apology. But why did you encourage me, if I may ask?'

There was a long silence. Finally, she said, 'Because I felt the need for someone . . . someone with me, in the house. You see, I was afraid . . . '

A small van darted unexpectedly in

front of us. I had to brake the car suddenly to avoid a collision. It was only a momentary thing, but by the time it was over, Maggie's train of thought seemed broken.

'Left at the next corner,' she directed me. I made the turn and saw just before us the familiar studio gates of Horizon Films. My emotions were mixed: excitement at being here; disappointment that I would not hear whatever it was Maggie had been about to say.

We stopped at the gate, but a glimpse of the car and its passenger was all we needed for admittance. The guard tipped his hat respectfully. 'Morning, Miss Berke,' he said.

'Good morning, George,' she replied graciously. 'How's the wife? And little Emory?'

He chuckled, glowing with pleasure. 'Little Emory, as you call him, has three little ones of his own now.'

She laughed too. 'Tell him he must bring them over to the house some day, and you come too.'

If I had ever doubted that Maggie still

retained star status, my doubts would have been erased with that visit. It seemed as if all work stopped, and everyone came to see Maggie — to chat with her if they were acquainted, and to stare if they were not.

C. R. Ross was directing a picture. I thought that Maggie was surely the only person in the world who would dare to call that famous person Charlie. If he minded, he kept the fact to himself. A chair was brought for Maggie, and she not only watched the shooting, but gave Ross her advice on a scene, which he accepted gratefully.

'And this lovely young thing,' he asked of me. 'If you ask me she ought to be a star herself.'

'My niece, Mari,' Maggie explained. 'She's decided against a movie career.'

'On advice of counsel,' I added.

He looked from Maggie to me. 'The trouble with Maggie,' he said, 'is that she's afraid someone else might become as big as she was.'

'Impossible,' Maggie said confidently.

Our tour of the studio was complete.

We not only watched the shooting, but I saw all of the behind-the-scenes activities that mark a major studio. I watched sets being painted by a man I later learned was a highly regarded serious artist. I was awed by the wardrobe department and the makeup facilities. I stood in the very dressing room that had been Maggie's, and was now still unoccupied.

'Who could take her place?' Ross asked.

The big back lot actually contained a small lake used for ocean settings, plus a western street that I had seen in more movies than I cared to remember, and a small town setting. New York was represented with another street.

And everywhere we went, Maggie's fans and friends followed. I stopped counting the autographs she signed, and many of them were for people who were stars in their own right, at least by contemporary standards.

It was late afternoon when Ross himself and the head of the studio, Sid Whalen, escorted us back to the car. I was exhausted, and I knew Maggie must have been too, but true to form she managed to look as fresh and unruffled as she had when we arrived.

I could not help contrasting this poised, self-assured woman with the despondent creature I had seen the night before. What great sorrow would be necessary to make Maggie Berke surrender her façade?

6

I did not often see Davis, the hired man. When I did, however, I was quite aware that he had not forgotten, nor forgiven, my interference. He made no attempt to disguise his resentful looks. It was also apparent that he was not afraid of getting fired as a result of his clash with me. He seemed smug and assured of himself. I wondered for a time if he had heard of Maggie's attitude toward the incident; or perhaps he was certain of his hold over Maggie. If he had such a hold.

The day after our visit to the studio I was suddenly witness to a scene that explained several things to me. I had come into the kitchen to deliver a message from Maggie to the inconspicuous Miss Wright. Miss Wright was not in the kitchen, but I noticed that the back door was open. Thinking perhaps that she had stepped outside, I crossed the room and stepped out.

Miss Wright was not outside, but Elisa

was. She was with Davis; very much with Davis, in fact. She was in his embrace, returning what was clearly a very ardent kiss.

I stepped back into the kitchen at once, without being seen. Careful to make as little noise as possible, I fled into the hall. There, I paused to reflect on what I had just seen.

Davis and Elisa were lovers, that much was obvious. I remembered then the night that I had seen Elisa furtively crossing the terrace. It should have been obvious to me then. Davis's apartment was over the garages; it could only have been to his rooms that she was going. This was why she had defended him in front of Maggie, and how he knew that Maggie had taken his part.

But did it explain his position here? Would Maggie tolerate his cruelty and his sloppy work only because he was the object of Elisa's affections? Perhaps Maggie suffered a subconscious guilt because Elisa had always been so out of her class. Perhaps she felt Elisa was entitled to whatever happiness she could have, at the price of a poor employee.

Of course, there was every reason to suppose that Maggie did not even know of the relationship between Elisa and Davis. I wondered how I might tactfully go about finding this out. Finally I thought that I might in casual conversation be able to learn the truth. I saw that I was interfering in what was, after all, Elisa's personal business and not mine. Still, I felt that there was a link between her intimacy with Davis and the strange atmosphere here in this house, and I set out to find Maggie.

Maggie was in her den, but as I came near, I realized she was not alone. I could hear the sound of her voice carrying clearly into the hall.

Ordinarily I would have thought nothing of this, but as I approached the door, I heard my name mentioned. So subtly had suspicion been planted in my mind that I instinctively stopped before I reached the open door.

' . . . but if Mari is in danger,' Maggie said, 'then I must do something.'

I heard no answering voice, and after a moment, Maggie went on, 'Oh, you don't understand. If only you realized how frightened I've been of late. I know the danger is real and present. I'm not just being a neurotic old woman. I'm certain of it. And I wanted Mari here. I thought she might be able to . . . to protect me. But if I've put her in any danger, well, don't you see, I will be responsible.'

I drew back, frightened and further puzzled by what I had heard. I would have gone away without hearing more, but just then I heard a noise from the kitchen, and realized that Elisa was coming in. If I remained here or tried to flee, I would reveal myself as an eavesdropper. I had no other alternative but to whirl about and, before Elisa made an appearance in the hall, walk into the library. I had on my lips an apology for my interruption. It was not needed, apparently. Maggie was alone.

'Why hello, dear,' she greeted me, smiling broadly.

'Hello,' I said, looking around the room. Yes, she was alone. And there was only the one entrance to the room, unless her companion had climbed out a

91

window. 'I thought I heard voices.'

Her innocent greeting had led me to think I must have been mistaken, but I had forgotten for a moment that Maggie was an actress. Now, for just a fraction of a second, the mask of the performer slipped, and she paled slightly.

'You embarrass me,' she said quickly. 'I feel so foolish, admitting that I talk to myself. It makes me sound like a doddering old fool.'

I smiled in response and said, 'As a matter of fact, I do the same thing myself. It's a silly habit, isn't it?'

In fact, I did not believe her. She had not spoken as one speaks to oneself. And even had she done so, the fleeting expression that had crossed Maggie's face told me that Maggie was hiding the truth.

But what was the truth? If someone had been here with Maggie, who was it, and where had he gone? I let my glance glide about the room again, but there was no telephone either, and no evidence of a tape recorder.

'Did you come in to tell me something?' Maggie asked. She had drawn herself up impressively.

'No,' I said, and then, 'Yes. I didn't find Miss Wright. Do you want me to leave a note for her?' I could not now bring up the subject of Elisa and Davis; I had heard a footstep in the hall outside. Elisa did not come in at once, however, and I realized that she was listening as I had listened a moment before.

'It isn't necessary,' Maggie said. 'I'll tell her myself when I see her later.'

As I started from the room, Elisa came into it. Her face was still flushed, and I felt my own face redden with my secret knowledge. I could not miss the ominous look she gave me. I nodded a greeting and went on by, into the hall. I was shivering. She had heard Maggie and me discuss Miss Wright, and she was intelligent enough to know that if I had been searching for Miss Wright, I would have been in the kitchen.

Her suspicions had been aroused, and that one look she had given me had asked what I had seen. My guilty reaction had given her the answer. She knew that I knew and she hated me bitterly for it.

I sought the safety of my own room. There I stood at the window and stared without seeing at the street scene below me.

I was frightened. I did not even know exactly of what, or why, but I could no longer ignore the impression of danger and malevolence around me, permeating the atmosphere in this place.

'All right,' I said aloud, trying to clear my confused thoughts, 'supposing that falling chandelier was not an accident. Just who would have caused it, and why?'

For some reason, Elisa hated me bitterly. But I could not believe she could wish real harm to me, and certainly not before she had truly met me, not the very moment I set foot in the house.

Davis resented me, but again, not before I had even come. He was resentful because I had scolded him for his cruelty to a stray dog and taken the story to Maggie. But this was hardly motive for violence.

And there was no one else. Unless . . . unless I took into consideration whomever Maggie had been talking to.

I spoke of these things that night at dinner with Ken.

'I'm not surprised,' he said when I told him what I had seen with Elisa and Davis. 'That explains his arrogance and his indifference toward his work, but it doesn't explain why Maggie should tolerate it.'

'Pity for Elisa?' I suggested.

He shook his head. 'It's just not like Maggie. No, there's something wrong there. Something centering around Maggie.'

I hesitated for a moment before saying, 'Ken, do you think . . . is Maggie all right mentally?'

'What makes you ask that?'

I explained briefly the conversation I had overheard before finding Maggie alone. 'I can't explain it,' I concluded. 'I was convinced that she was talking to someone else; or, that she *thought* she was talking to someone else.'

He frowned and sipped at his cocktail. After a pause he said, 'Elisa has already talked to me about the same subject. About Maggie's mental health, that is.'

My pulse quickened. 'You mean she's suggested Maggie might not be well?'

He nodded. 'She's asked me about the requirements for having someone committed.'

My shock was unconcealed. 'Ken, you can't mean that. Of course Maggie has been acting strangely, I'll admit that. But that doesn't make her crazy, or in need of confinement. You don't think Maggie's crazy, do you?'

'I wish I knew,' he said. I started to argue, but he silenced me with a gesture. 'You see, I already knew about Maggie talking to herself.'

'Then it's happened before? And Elisa heard her. But still . . . '

'Maggie doesn't think she's talking to herself,' he said, interrupting me gently. 'She believes she's talking to her son, Buddy.'

'Buddy?' I looked bewildered. 'But . . . '

'She believes he comes back to see her. She claims to see him and talk to him.'

I sat for a moment in stunned silence. I thought of the night Maggie had seen me on the stairs and mistaken me for someone else. I thought of her disappointment on discovering it was me and not who she expected. She had expected Buddy then; it explained her behavior. And it explained her talking to herself.

It was a peculiar situation, and certainly a tragic one: Maggie, alone, with only Elisa and her memories in that big, gloomy house. If ever one was going to believe in ghosts it would be in that house, with its shadows. I saw Maggie haunted by the past, haunted so painfully that the past actually came to life for her in the form of her dead son.

But did that render Maggie insane? I did not think so. Yet I felt again the sense of foreboding that I had experienced of late, a feeling of impending doom, and I knew that it would never again be quite the same between Maggie and me.

7

The subject of Maggie's sanity and her possible confinement put a damper on the evening. 'I'm afraid I don't feel much in the mood for dancing,' I apologized to Ken on the way home.

'Now don't let it worry you,' he said firmly. 'That's my job. I probably shouldn't have said anything at all to you.'

'No,' I said, 'I'm glad you did. I'm no psychiatrist, of course, but I certainly ought to be able to tell if a person acts like they aren't in full possession of their mental faculties.'

'Good idea,' he agreed. 'I don't mind admitting that this has been a big weight on my shoulders. I like Maggie Berke. When I was just a little kid my mother raved about Maggie. She was her idol, and I grew up thinking of Maggie as slightly more elevated than God.'

I understood what he meant, and I knew Ken was sincere in his concern. If

I could assure him that it was not necessary, I knew he would resist Elisa's efforts.

'The one thing that bothers me,' I said, 'is why Elisa should be the one to bring this up.'

'You're forgetting the possibility that she might be sincere,' Ken said.

'Yes,' I admitted. 'But if she isn't right, if Maggie is quite sane, then what motive would Elisa have to make anyone think otherwise?'

'There's the house, of course,' he said. 'And the money. Maggie was notoriously wise in her investments when she was a big star. Even after all these years she's worth a bundle, according to all accounts.'

'But Elisa has those now, in effect if not in fact,' I said. 'She already lives in the house, with complete freedom. She obviously has no limitations put on her way of life or her spending. I hardly think Maggie curtails her in any manner. Why have Maggie put away just so that she can go on living exactly as she is now?'

'Assuming that she would,' he said. 'For all you know, Elisa may have dreams of joining the jet set.'

The suggestion brought a grin to my face for the first time in over an hour.

'Seriously,' Ken said, 'we're being unfair to Elisa in assuming right off the top that she has some wicked ulterior motive. She did nothing more than remark to me that Maggie has been acting strangely, and asked if I thought her mind might be going off. I promised to observe Maggie and give her my opinion in the future.'

'But Elisa believes in the ghost too,' I said suddenly. A succession of remembered scenes flitted through my consciousness. 'That first day I arrived, the chandelier came crashing down, almost on my head. And Elisa said something like, 'I knew there would be trouble if she came.' And later, I overheard her saying to Maggie, 'I told you he wouldn't like having her here.' Who else could she have meant but Buddy?'

'Davis, maybe? Maybe he knew you would discover that he and Elisa were sweethearts.'

'And he sent a chandelier down on my head to prevent my finding that out?' I asked with a trace of sarcasm.

'You're right, it is a bit thin,' he

admitted. 'Which brings us back to the only logical explanation. Elisa is sincere in her concern for Maggie's well-being.'

I doubted that Elisa was concerned for anybody's well-being but her own, but I did not say so aloud.

As it turned out, I was not finished with the subject of ghosts for the night. It was still early when I arrived back at the house. Ken did not come in but kissed me a warm good-night at the door.

'See you tomorrow,' he said, waiting until I had gone in before he left.

A light in the den told me Maggie was still up. As I came down the hall, she appeared in the doorway. She looked tired and drawn, and it took no skilled eye to see that something was troubling her.

'Darling,' she said, greeting me with a wan smile. 'I was just about to have a nightcap. Why don't you join me?' Almost as an afterthought she added, 'Elisa's here too. We'll all have one.'

Elisa looked anything but enthusiastic to have me join them, but she got up quietly and poured brandies for each of us, thrusting mine rudely into my hand.

'How was dinner?' Maggie asked brightly.

'Fine. Ken took me to the Swiss Chalet. It's a charming place.'

'Yes, one of my favorites.' After an awkward pause, she asked, 'You've become quite fond of Ken, haven't you?' When I blushed and nodded, she said, 'I can well imagine he would turn any girl's head with no difficulty.'

'I have some stiff competition, though,' I told her. 'He's positively wild about you.'

'Oh, what nonsense,' she said, but I could see that the flattery had cheered her. For a moment the lines of tension were gone from her face. It was fleeting, however. She seemed suddenly to remember her unhappiness, and her face sagged.

'Maggie,' I said impulsively, too concerned to be tactful. 'What is it — what's troubling you?' I leaned forward to clasp her hand in mine.

She sighed and met my gaze openly. 'I suppose it's no good going on hiding things from you.'

'I wonder if it's wise to bring all of one's personal business out into the open,' Elisa said sharply.

'Since it's my personal business,' Maggie retorted, 'I think I'm the one to decide that.' She rose and walked to the window, gazing out with her back to me. 'Mari,' she said finally, without turning, 'do you believe in . . . in life after the grave?'

'I believe,' I said slowly, 'that life as a quality is unending; that it goes on unbroken and unchanged, eternally, permeating everything that is.'

She turned swiftly, a smile breaking on her lips, but I went on before she could speak. 'But I believe that life as an individual experience is temporary. I think that the life within us is permanent, but our consciousness of it and our participation in it begins with birth and ends with death.'

She frowned as she thought over this. 'But when we die, in lieu of a better term, does the consciousness, the individual mind, the personality — do they all cease entirely? Might they not linger on too, in some way?'

'That,' I said, 'suggests a multitude of individual lives having no relationship to one another, rather than one life in which we share.' I shrugged, not wanting to sound too adamant. 'Of course, that's strictly a matter of one's personal beliefs. I daresay there's only one way either of us will know for sure, and that's to go through it.'

'Perhaps,' she said. I gave her a puzzled look. 'Suppose someone else went through it,' she said, 'and told us about it. Then we would know, would we not?'

'You mean, if someone came back from the grave?' I said, studying her carefully. 'Like, a ghost?'

She had become increasingly agitated during this conversation, and now her eyes widened and her face reflected her excitement. 'But suppose someone did come back — someone we knew and loved and trusted. Wouldn't that prove everything?'

'I don't know what it would prove. If we did see, or thought we saw, a ghost of someone we knew, it might just as well be a hallucination, or something of that sort. Or even a ruse on the part of someone else. It's accepting a great deal to say unequivocally that it is life after death.'

Maggie drew her shoulders back to deliver her announcement. 'I have seen Buddy's spirit.'

'That can't be,' I said in a voice that sounded unlike my own. 'Buddy's been dead for twenty years.'

'But that's the point, isn't it?' she asked. 'Oh, Mari, it's true. He comes back. He visits me here, in this house. He talks to me; he tells me things.' She was begging, despite her haughty pose — begging me to believe her. 'He's here constantly, all the time. He says he'll never leave again. Not so long as I live.'

'But I've never seen him,' I said. 'If he were here all the time, surely I would have bumped into him by now.'

'He doesn't like you,' Elisa said in a low voice from the chair in which she had remained seated. 'He didn't want you to come.'

I wanted to say something to her, but her words had set Maggie off again. 'Oh, that's all a mistake,' she said, wringing her hands pathetically. 'He doesn't understand, that's all. I've tried to get him to see that Mari's not an enemy; that she's a friend to me. Why won't he understand that?'

'Now, don't get yourself all upset,' Elisa

said, jumping up to rush to Maggie's side. Again I had the unpleasant experience of watching Maggie literally crumble into Elisa's arms.

'But why does he hate her so?' she whimpered, resting her cheek against Elisa's ample shoulder.

'There, there,' Elisa said, patting her and guiding her to the sofa. She gave me a frosty look over Maggie's head.

'Do you believe in this . . . this spirit?' I asked Elisa bluntly.

'Yes,' she said. She turned her back on me to assist Maggie into a chair. 'There, you just sit here and be quiet, and I'll get your pills. I told you it wouldn't do to upset yourself. I think she ought to be left alone,' she said to me as she started from the room.

I followed close on her heels, not satisfied yet with her answers. 'Do you mean to tell me,' I asked in the hall, 'that you have actually seen the ghost of her dead son?'

'The doctor told me to pamper her,' she said with a cold little smile playing upon her lips. 'You just saw for yourself how it upsets her to be contradicted on the matter.'

'But you don't believe that it's real?'

'I believe she thinks he is real,' she said stubbornly. 'And isn't that the important thing with a woman in her state of mind?' With that she turned her back on me and hurried away down the hall after Maggie's pills.

I was left alone to stare disconsolately after her. I did not have to ask what she considered Maggie's state of mind to be. I had seen for myself that she had deliberately encouraged Maggie in her fantasies, even to the point of lying about having seen a ghost. I could not help but wonder in how many ways Elisa had contributed to Maggie's 'state of mind.'

8

I had scarcely gotten to my own room and undressed for bed when the sound of screams rent the night. It was Maggie's voice, distorted by terror. I dashed from my room into the hall. There was no one in sight, but the screams had come from the direction of Maggie's room and I raced toward their source, hardly able to imagine what had caused her fright.

Before I reached her room, Elisa came out, closing the door firmly after her. She stopped squarely in my path, plainly intending to prevent my entering Maggie's bedroom. I paused before her.

'What happened?' I demanded breathlessly. 'I heard Maggie screaming.'

'She's all right,' Elisa told me. 'Go back to your room and leave this to me.'

I was shocked and angered. 'I will not,' I replied. 'Something's happened. Maggie sounded frightened to death. I'm her niece. If anything's wrong, I have a right to know what it is.'

She did not budge, however. She stood with her feet planted firmly apart. I could not get around her, and it looked as if the only way I would get into Maggie's room was by forcing Elisa out of my way. Considering her bulk and formidable appearance, that didn't seem a likely prospect.

As it turned out, I was spared that necessity. The door suddenly opened behind her and Maggie appeared. She looked whiter than a sheet and her breath was rapid and uneven. She had obviously overheard our quarrel. To my surprise, she took Elisa's side in it.

'Everything's all right,' she said, looking straight at me. I moved as though to come into the room, but she swung the door partly shut. 'It was nothing,' she insisted. 'I thought I saw something.'

I could see that she was trembling. 'I don't believe you,' I told her bluntly.

She sighed and for a moment I thought she would faint. Elisa seemed to think so too, for she moved closer as if to put a supporting arm around her. Maggie rallied enough to pull her shoulders back and remain in control of herself.

'Go to your room,' she said, in a tone that brooked no further objection. 'I'll come along there in a few moments and explain.'

The look of triumph on Elisa's face was hard to bear, but I knew that further argument was useless. 'Very well,' I said. I turned quickly and went back along the hall to my own room. I sat on the edge of the bed, waiting for Maggie to come, and wondering what might possibly have frightened her so badly.

It was nearly half an hour before Maggie knocked lightly at my door and came into the room. I had almost decided to go to her room again when she made her appearance. She was calm now, at least relatively so, and I saw that she had taken time to freshen her makeup and comb her hair. I had an impression that she was on stage, prepared to play a part for my benefit, and I was puzzled.

She flashed one of her silver-screen smiles at me. 'Mari, it's been such a pleasure to me, having you here.'

Something in the way she said that gave me pause. 'That sounded as though I'm going to be leaving soon,' I said, not in any mood for sparring.

'I'm sorry, dear,' she said, looking quite as sad and wearied as she had in several of her best movies. 'But I do think perhaps that would be best.'

'But why?' I asked, jumping up from the bed. 'Because of your . . . your visits from Buddy?'

A flicker of genuine emotion lighted her eyes briefly. 'Then you do believe . . . ?' She left the question unanswered. Then: 'Did you know that Doctor Wolfe and Elisa have been planning to have me put away, in an asylum of one sort or another?'

I could think of nothing to say, but my expression must have told her the truth. She nodded with a wry smile. 'That was one of my reasons for wanting you to come here,' she said. 'I thought as a relative perhaps you would see things a bit differently.'

'Elisa's a relative,' I said.

'Not by blood,' she said. 'She's only a stepdaughter, although certainly she has been kind to me over the years that we've lived here in this big, lonely house together. She truly has been like a daughter.'

'But if you suspect . . . ' I began.

'Hasn't Ken Wolfe discussed it with you?' she asked frankly.

I could not lie to her. 'Yes,' I whispered.

'And don't you see,' she went on, 'how things have been altered? Your falling in love with Ken has changed everything. It puts everyone in a difficult position. For that reason, I think it best that you plan to return home. Oh, you needn't leave this minute. I think within the next few days, say a week on the outside.'

I had completely succumbed to her spell. So well had she played her part that in only a moment I had forgotten that she was playing a part, delivering a well-rehearsed script. But she was out of practice. A gesture — the mere wave of a hand — rang falsely, and I was jarred back to reality.

'Maggie,' I said, angry again for having been tricked, 'you're lying to me. That isn't your reason at all. Something happened tonight in your room, something that frightened you enough to make you ask me to leave. And I think I have a right to know what that something was.' The sweet, sad look left her face. I knew I had been right. 'Let me help,' I begged, coming to her to put a hand gently on one frail shoulder. 'I want to help, really I do, if you'll only trust me.'

To my surprise, she sank into my arms, leaning wearily against me. I felt her slim body begin to shake as the sobbing started. 'You have to go,' she cried against my shoulder. 'I've been warned.'

I guided her to the bed and sat down with her. When she had begun to grow calm again, I said, 'What do you mean, you've been warned? By whom? Elisa?'

'No, no, don't you understand? By Buddy.'

For a moment I was too shocked to answer. 'You're right,' I said finally. 'I certainly don't understand. What did he say? And why should he want me to leave anyway, for Heaven's sake?'

'He didn't want you to come,' she said wearily. 'He warned me then, but I thought he was just being jealous. I told him you were a friend, and I thought that once you came and he saw that you really meant well by me — well, I thought he'd change his mind. But then you got here, and the chandelier . . . '

'Do you think he did that?' I asked sharply.

'Why of course,' she said, her eyes innocently wide. 'He told me afterward that he did. And he warned me again about letting you stay.'

'Tell me,' I said, 'when Buddy warns you, does he appear to you, or just what?'

'Sometimes. Sometimes he talks to me, even when I'm asleep. And sometimes . . . ' She suddenly grew frightened again, remembering something. She jumped to her feet, as pale as before. 'Go to my room,' she said. 'Then you'll understand.'

I stood too, frightened by this sudden change. But I knew that if I were to really help Maggie, I must know what it was that I was combating. 'I'll be right back,' I said, hurrying toward the hall. 'You wait here.' I closed the door securely after me and went quickly down the hall.

At first I thought she must have been hallucinating. There were no shadowy figures lurking in the corners, no phantom heads floating through the air. Then I saw the mirror over the dresser.

'Mari must leave, or everyone will suffer the consequences.' It was written in a childish scrawl, in what at first appeared to be blood. I must admit that it sent a shiver along my spine.

I forced myself to step into the room and cross to the dresser. I put out a finger and rubbed away part of one letter. Lipstick.

'Not very inspired,' I said to myself, 'for a ghost.'

Elisa had come upstairs for Maggie's pills earlier. It would have taken only a minute to scrawl this warning and leave it to be discovered when she brought Maggie up a short time later. Poor hysterical Maggie, so convinced by this time of her haunting that she could not even see through a ruse as flimsy as this one.

I was not going to be so easily tricked, however. I opened a drawer to find Maggie's makeup collection. I even found what seemed to be the very lipstick that had been used for the writing.

After a moment, I went back down the hall to my own room. Maggie looked around anxiously as I came in. 'You see why I was so frightened,' she said. 'There's no telling what he'll do to you — to all of us. He's still only a child, you see, even after all this time.'

'I think you'd better come back to your room,' I said calmly. She gave me a curious look. 'There's something you had better see for yourself,' I added.

She came with me. In the hall, I said, 'I think Elisa had better come too.'

Still looking at me in a puzzled way, Maggie knocked at Elisa's door, and when she appeared, asked her to come with us to her bedroom.

'Has something happened?' Elisa wanted to know.

'Yes,' I said. 'Something that seems quite significant to me.'

I opened the door to Maggie's bedroom and stepped aside for the two of them to enter. They gasped in unison as their eyes went at once to the mirror.

I came in after them, looking in that direction also. The second message looked as if it, too, had been written in blood. 'Mother,' it said, 'I did not write that. There is someone else here trying to fool you.'

9

'Elisa,' Maggie cried, running across to stare at the message up close. 'Look. I knew it; I knew Buddy couldn't be so hateful.'

I turned away from the violent look Elisa shot me. There was no doubt that she knew who had written this second message, just as I knew who had written the first. I had declared war, fighting fire with fire. I had also gained a bitter enemy, and this was an uneven contest because I did not even know what the purpose of it was, while presumably she did.

'Isn't it wonderful, Elisa?' Maggie said again, coming back to us. 'Oh, Mari,' she said, hugging me delightedly. 'You don't have to go. Buddy wants you here. He must. Else why would he go to the trouble to reveal the truth to us? And to think,' she went on, turning again to Elisa. 'To think, all this time we've let ourselves be taken in by an imposter, only pretending to be Buddy.'

'I wonder,' Elisa said coldly. She went to the mirror and stared hard at the glass, as though willing the message to disappear. I almost expected it to respond to her withering gaze. 'This does show that there is more than one presence here. But it doesn't tell us which is the imposter, and which is really Buddy.'

I saw Maggie's joy flee as quickly as it had come. 'But do you think the first message is from Buddy after all?'

'I don't see how that could be,' I said, jumping into the fray. 'Why would an imposter write that second message? It makes sense only if it really comes from Buddy. Who else would have any reason?'

'An interesting question,' Elisa said quietly. For a brief instant those cruel eyes were slicing me to ribbons. When they shifted to Maggie, however, they were once again muted and soft. 'There's one way to clear this mystery up,' she said.

'How is that?' I asked, uneasily. She was showing too much confidence, I thought.

'Madame Divina,' Maggie said softly.

Elisa nodded sagely.

'Who is that?' I asked, but I had already begun to suspect what the answer would be.

'A medium,' Elisa answered.

'Maggie,' I said, arguing desperately while victory ebbed from between my fingers like so much fine sand. 'You surely aren't going to resort to that sort of hocus-pocus. You've had a clear message from Buddy. Isn't that enough for you?'

'If it *was* from Buddy,' Elisa said smugly, aware that she had regained the upper hand. 'And Madame Divina is no charlatan engaging in hocus-pocus. She's a very fine medium — one who can work miracles.'

'Yes, that's true,' Maggie agreed. 'We've used her before, darling, when we had to summon Buddy up at a specific time rather than waiting for him to come at his leisure. Madame Divina has almost instant contact with the other side, especially with Buddy. In fact, it was he himself who suggested her to us in one of his messages.'

'Written on a mirror?' I asked, unable to resist the dig.

'No, he spoke to me in my sleep,'

Maggie replied. 'I think Madame Divina is exactly the answer, Elisa,' she said. 'Tomorrow you will arrange for a séance. But it must be done here, in the house.'

'Madame's schedule is quite full,' Elisa said with a cluck of her tongue. 'She might not be able to arrange anything on such short notice.'

'Nonsense.' Maggie waved her hand imperiously. 'We'll pay any expenses. This is an emergency. Tell her. Explain about all this.' She indicated the mirror.

'Yes, she'll be interested in this turn of events,' Elisa agreed.

I made one last stab. 'Maggie, I don't like this. Are you sure it's wise?'

'Now, now,' Maggie said, once more in charge of the situation. 'This way we'll know. Now you just go on back to your room and rest easy. It's been an exciting night, but tomorrow we'll have this mystery cleared up. If there has been some mischief-maker at work, then there's no reason for you to go. Buddy will tell us what to do.'

There was nothing I could do but accept Maggie's verdict and return to my own room. It was late into the night before I could sleep.

When I woke in the morning, the day loomed ominously before me. I was convinced that Madame Divina was not only a charlatan, but an accomplice in whatever scheme Elisa was furthering.

I skipped breakfast, took only coffee, and went out immediately afterward. I wanted to talk to Ken, but I did not want to do it from the house. I was all too aware of Elisa's hovering presence, and once or twice I had gotten the impression that she was keeping a close eye on me. Nor did I overlook the satisfaction with which she announced, coming into the breakfast room while Maggie and I were having coffee, 'It's all arranged. Madame Divina will arrive at nine tonight. We're to have everything set up in the usual fashion.'

'You'll find this most revealing,' Maggie said to me.

'No doubt,' was all I could say.

'Unless,' Elisa suggested with a faint smile on her lips, 'you would prefer not to be here. Some people are frightened by this sort of thing.'

'I wouldn't miss it for the world,' I assured her.

Ken was not in when I first called his office. 'Can I have him return your call?' the secretary wanted to know.

'No, I'll call him again,' I told her. I was in a coffee shop phone booth.

I got him on my third try. 'I've got appointments stacked one on top of the other,' he said sadly when I explained I wanted to see him.

'This is important,' I said. 'It's about the difficulties at the house.'

He hesitated only a moment before saying, 'Come by my office. I'll find time.'

In a neat, spotless examining room he listened patiently while I brought him up to date on the events of the previous evening. He made no interruptions, although his eyebrows shot up when I told him of the message written on the mirror, and he grinned boyishly at my response to that difficulty.

'So they've set up a ghost hunt for tonight,' he said when I had concluded. He frowned and shook his head. 'I don't like this. It sounds to me like these people are up to no good. And by now they also know you're on to them. Those warnings may not have come from any spirit world, but they might be valid just the same.'

'What can I do though?' I asked. 'If I don't show up for the séance, it will leave Elisa a clear hand.'

'Maybe if I showed up?' he offered.

I had thought of that possibility myself, but I knew it was only wishful thinking on my part. 'They'd know why you were there.' I sighed and stood. 'No, it seems there's not a thing I can do but be there for this séance and keep my eyes open for any tricks.'

'If this Madame Divina has had any real experience, you probably won't spot her tricks,' he said. 'These people can be pretty sharp.'

'I've one thing in my favor,' I said. 'So far they've only had to fool Maggie, and no doubt she was more than half willing to be deceived. It may have made them a little careless.'

The day seemed to crawl past. I knew it was hopeless even to try to eat dinner, and pleading a headache, I spent the early part of the evening in my room. Again Elisa had an advantage over me; she knew what the evening held in store, while I could only guess, with each guess making me more apprehensive.

It was time at last. Maggie came to tap on my door. 'Madame Divina is here,' she said. 'We're ready to begin whenever you join us.'

'I'll be right there,' I said. I paused to look at myself in the mirror. I looked frightened. Stubbornly I pulled my shoulders back, determined to keep my lack of confidence a secret.

Finally, looking less concerned than I felt, I left my room and started downstairs, toward my first séance.

10

Madame Divina was a caricature of every medium I had ever read about or seen in movies. She was long and thin, with her jet-black hair pulled severely back from a gaunt face. Her eyes were small and dark and constantly mobile, and her hands seemed taloned. She gave me a guarded look as I came into the parlor.

'How do you do?' I said when Maggie introduced us. I offered my hand but she ignored it.

'Do you believe?' she demanded coldly.

I shrugged the question off. 'I don't know,' I said. 'I've never attended anything like this before. But I don't specifically disbelieve, if that's what you mean.' I sensed an attempt to excuse me from the proceedings, and I fully intended to remain in the room.

She yielded begrudgingly. 'The spirits will know,' she muttered, and turned her back on me.

The furniture had been moved back against the walls to clear the center of the room. A large, round game table had been placed there, with four chairs about it. It was bare except for a large crystal ball in the center. Candles gleamed in candelabra about the room. The spirits, it seemed, were put off by anything so modern as electricity.

'Miss Wright declined to join us,' Maggie said. 'So there'll only be the four of us.'

At Madame Divina's instructions we seated ourselves in the chairs. 'You must clasp hands with one another,' she said, taking Maggie's hand in one of hers and Elisa's in the other. I was across from the medium, between Elisa and Maggie. 'Do not break the circle, no matter what might happen. This is important for our safety. I repeat, do not break the chain. Also, do not speak until I tell you it is correct to do so.'

The flickering candles gave only a dim, eerie light to the big room. The shadows that retreated from the glow actually seemed to be alive. I thought I could see

127

them writhing impatiently in the corners.

'Silence,' Madame Divina commanded sharply, although in fact no one had been speaking. 'Make your minds clear. Rid them of all thoughts, all confusion. We are at peace, attuned to the vast universe. We are free of the world and its confusions, and we now become one with all that is, that has been, and that will be. Feel this. Sense it travelling through your being. Let go. Let go.'

She spoke in a hypnotic tone, punctuating her commands with a sharply raised voice. Despite my intention of remaining on guard, I actually found myself relaxing, absorbing her instructions. My mind drifted. I had a sense of peace and relaxation.

I jerked my head suddenly upright. The voice was droning on and on, repeating its instructions to relax, to let go. I had nearly fallen asleep, into a hypnotic trance. I glanced sideways. All of their heads were lowered. Maggie seemed actually to have gone into a trance. I could not tell whether the others had done so or not. Elisa's fingers clasped mine firmly. On the other side, Maggie held that hand more gently in hers.

' . . . free of all tensions,' Madame Divina was saying. 'Perfectly relaxed. Deeply immersed in the realm of the spirit. Deep, deep, deep . . . '

Again I struggled with the realization that I was falling asleep. My eyes sprang open. For a moment I could not identify the change in the atmosphere; then I saw that the candles on the nearest table had gone out. We were in what was nearly darkness. Only the candles on the distant tables shed a faint glow across us. How had the candles gone out? The wind? Someone's breath? Had they been snuffed? I really did not know. The near darkness made the scene still more eerie.

' . . . we call upon you, O spirits. Come.' It was a low voice, but firm, seeming to demand obedience. 'We call upon the spirits of the other realms. We call upon you to present yourselves if you are here. Manifest yourselves before us. We command it. Appear before us; speak to us; make your presence known.'

The room seemed strangely oppressive,

as if it were closing in upon me. The air was thick and I seemed to smell the exotic scent of incense, but I could not recall any being burned. I had an urge to stand, to break the circle. I restrained myself. I had to go through with this, for Maggie's sake. Also, I had a scheme of my own, if the opportunity to use it presented itself. I did not want to admit a further fact: the weird scene had a strange, morbid fascination about it.

'Yes, yes, we feel your presence,' Madame Divina cried aloud. 'You are real, you are near, we feel you. Why do you not speak to us? Give us a sign of your presence. Knock once for yes, twice for no . . . ' She paused and then asked, 'Tell us if you are present.'

There was a long, pregnant silence. Then came a sharp rap. Once, signifying yes. The wind seemed to beat a tattoo against a window pane. A curtain billowed. I vaguely wondered why a window had been left open, but my mind was occupied with the dialogue going on at the table. It was only suggestion, of course, and yet I actually sensed something, as though there really were an alien presence in the room. I could see how effectively Maggie had been duped. Madame Divina was an expert. How had she caused the knocking? I wondered. Had she and Elisa broken the chain? In the darkness I couldn't tell.

'We come to you with an urgent question,' Madame Divina went on. 'It is a question that troubles us much; that only you can answer for us. There is a visitor here, a stranger to this house. Do you know who I mean?'

Again there was a yes answer, a single knock.

'She has been warned to leave. She has been warned that she is in danger here. Is she in danger?'

Another single knock.

'Should she leave?'

Another single knock. I had decided what I must do, and I was alert now. I could not free my hands without giving myself away, but my shoes had metal plates on them. With my legs crossed, I could just manage to hit the bottom of the table. I kicked twice, signifying a no answer. To my delight, the knocks sounded similar in tone to the previous ones.

There was a long silence. I heard Elisa suck in her breath sharply. Her hand tightened involuntarily on mine, and she looked quickly in my direction to be sure Maggie still held my other hand. I pretended not to see her.

Madame Divina seemed disconcerted by this confusion. 'There were two different answers,' Maggie said in a stunned whisper.

'Silence,' Madame Divina snapped. 'O spirit,' she cried loudly, 'tell us, is there more than one of you present?'

There were two quick taps, a no answer. I waited a moment and then tapped once with my shoe.

Again there was a long silence. We were at an impasse. I was determined to continue contradicting every answer as long as the séance lasted. I felt certain they hadn't rigged any visual gimmicks or they would have resorted to them by now . . . and I knew from Maggie's excited glances about the table that I had succeeded in my goal of convincing her of the presence of more than one spirit. As for Elisa and Madame Divina, I had hardly expected to convince them.

Elisa was more resourceful than I had bargained for, however. The silence was broken by her mournful groaning. At first I thought she meant to fool Maggie into believing that it was one of the spirits, and I was confident Maggie would see through anything so transparent. I had forgotten that séances sometimes included possession by an allegedly departed spirit.

'She's going into a trance,' Madame Divina declared with an unmistakable note of triumph. 'Silence, please. We mustn't endanger her.'

'Ohhh,' Elisa moaned, rolling her head from side to side.

'Speak,' Madame Divina commanded. I resisted an urge to give Elisa a violent kick.

'Mother.' It was a lower voice than the one Elisa normally used. I had to admit she was good at this. Her tone sounded hollow and appropriately sepulcher-ish. 'Mother.'

'Yes, yes, I'm here,' Maggie cried

breathlessly, leaning across the table. 'Buddy, is that you? Is it really you, and not some imposter?'

'Yes, it is I, mother,' Elisa moaned. 'I've come to warn you . . . warn you . . . make Mari leave. She is in danger. She is in danger. Make . . . leave . . . '

'Oh, but Buddy,' Maggie said. 'Won't you let me explain to you?'

Again I had that sense of oppression. I fought against it. We were at a crucial moment, and I dared not lose my wits now. My head was actually throbbing. Something was happening, but I couldn't define just what. It seemed increasingly difficult to breathe.

'Must go, at once . . . ' Elisa was repeating in a faltering tone. 'Danger if she stays . . . '

There was a sudden shattering of glass. Something had broken a window. The wind rushed through the room with what seemed a hurricane force, extinguishing the candles. Someone screamed; Maggie, I thought. My hands were freed. Elisa had jumped to her feet. I scrambled up too but in the blackness I could see nothing.

Something brushed my face. The curtains, I thought, billowing in the wind. Maggie screamed again, and someone swore. My heart pounded violently in my breast, and I nearly screamed myself.

It was only a moment before Elisa had found the light switch and plunged us into brightness again. My first thought was that for someone so recently in a trance she certainly seemed in full possession of her faculties. But she was alarmed too, I saw, as was Madame Divina. I went to Maggie and put an arm about her; she was trembling violently.

A branch had fallen from a tree and crashed through the terrace window. It lay half in, half out of the room. I knew from the expressions of Elisa and Madame Divina that this had not been part of their act. Providence, it seemed, had intervened and delivered me a stroke of luck.

11

It was Maggie who recovered her sense of decorum long enough to summon Miss Wright. 'I'm afraid we've had an accident here,' she said when that pale creature came, a bit nervously, I thought, into the room. 'Would you look after this, and ask Davis to do something about the window?'

We adjourned to the library, Elisa and Madame Divinia looking still nonplussed. Elisa was not one, however, to let grass grow under the feet of her scheme.

'At any rate,' she said flatly as we came into the library, 'we got our questions answered. You are in danger,' she said to me. 'And it was quite clear that you ought to leave, the sooner the better.'

'I'm surprised you remember all that so clearly, what with being in a trance,' I replied, at the same time looking for some sort of argument with which to counter her statements.

Surprisingly, it was Maggie who found it for me. 'I'm not at all sure,' she said thoughtfully, pausing in the act of pouring brandy for each of us.

'The spirit spoke through Elisa,' Madame Divina said. 'We all heard her. We know she was in a trance. The spirit does not lie. The voice said the intruder must go.'

'Yes,' Maggie agreed, handing around the glasses. 'But which spirit was it? That's the central question, isn't it?'

'Why, it was Buddy. He said so,' Elisa said, taken aback by this turn of events. She was not, I was certain, accustomed to having Maggie question the results of these little sessions of theirs.

'True, he said so,' Maggie said. 'But does that make it so? Or was this another imposter? Because we have had an imposter along the way. And I have to say, we don't know yet which one spoke.'

'That's right,' I said quickly. 'There were two messages before, on the mirror. And two sets of answers to the questions Madame Divina asked. We still have no way of knowing which spirit is Buddy's

137

and which is the intruder.'

'That is so,' Madame Divina said begrudgingly. I had won this round and she knew it.

'I suppose so,' Elisa admitted. After a moment, however, she added, 'But, if something should happen, something awful, then we'd know. Only, then it might be too late. It might be too late for you.' She said this directly to me, and I needed no special insight to recognize the warning implicit in her words. I might have won this particular round, but I had also won powerful enemies for myself. I sipped my brandy gratefully. I felt in need of its vitalizing influence.

Later, alone in my room, I found myself pondering the position in which I had placed myself in the house. I no longer doubted that, for whatever reason, Elisa was my enemy, and Maggie's. I was also fully aware that Davis, as her sweet-heart, would be Elisa's ally. In the game of wits we were playing, I was matched against the two of them.

Maggie, of course, meant me no harm, but she was unaware of the struggle that was going on about her. Even if I could make her aware of the fact that she was in some way in danger, and that the danger emanated from Elisa, I could hardly regard Maggie as an ally. It was I who would have to protect her. The only other occupant of the house was Miss Wright, who slept and, for the most part, lived in a little room behind the kitchen. I doubted that she would be of much assistance in any crisis.

Of course there was Ken; his help I knew I could count on. He could not always be here, however, and there was no telling when Elisa would decide to make a move.

I was reminded of this thought before the night was over, when the knock came at my door. I was in deep sleep, so that the rapping had to be repeated several times before I wakened fully.

'Who's there?' I asked finally, sitting up in bed and reaching for my robe.

'It's Elisa,' she called from the hall. 'Is Maggie in there?'

'Maggie? Good Heavens no,' I answered, slipping out of bed and thrusting my arms into the sleeves of the robe as I hurried across the room. I opened the door to find Elisa there in her nightdress. 'What is it, what's happened?'

'Maggie's not in her room,' she said.

Instinctively I glanced toward my wrist, but of course my watch was on the nightstand. 'It's three in the morning,' Elisa informed me.

Fear gripped me. I went past her and ran down the hall to Maggie's room. The door was open, the room empty.

'I told you she wasn't there,' Elisa said, having followed me more slowly.

I recalled the night I had discovered Maggie wandering about downstairs, the night she mistook me for Buddy. 'Have you searched the house?' I asked.

'I called from the stairs. There was no answer.'

Something crossed my mind. 'Why were you looking for her anyway at this hour of night?'

'I thought I heard something. When I came into the hall I noticed that there was a light on in her room. I thought perhaps she was having difficulty sleeping, so I went along and knocked on her door. When she didn't answer, I went in and discovered that she wasn't there. Naturally I wondered where she could be. It's quite late. But there were no lights downstairs.'

'She sometimes goes about in the dark,' I said, going toward the stairs. 'Didn't you know that?'

'No,' she said. 'Usually I take sleeping draughts. I'm rarely awake during the night.'

'But you are tonight,' I said, thinking that her sleeping draughts provided her with a convenient alibi during those times Maggie thought she saw or heard her dead child's ghost in those dark rooms downstairs.

'I was busy thinking over the séance,' she said, following me down the stairs. 'I often stay awake after one of those events.'

And probably plotting new mischief, I thought to myself.

'Maggie?' I called, flicking on the lights in the downstairs hall. There was no reply. I went into the den, turning on those lights too. 'Maggie?'

With Elisa trailing behind me I went from room to room, turning on lights as we went, and calling Maggie's name. There was no reply and no sign of Maggie.

'We'd better check the employees,' I said, moving toward the kitchen door.

'I'll check with Davis,' she said.

'Perhaps we'd better both go,' I said. 'If anything has happened, it might be best if we were together.'

Whatever she thought of my suggestion, she acquiesced. Davis answered our knock almost immediately — too quickly, I thought, for a man who was sound asleep.

'She ain't here,' he said when we explained why we had come.

'I didn't expect that she would be,' I assured him, trying not to show that his cold looks still frightened me. 'But I did think perhaps you might have heard or seen something that would give us a clue.'

'Not me. I comes up here to my room and I calls it a day. I mind my own business.'

'I'm sure you do,' I said stiffly. He

started to close his door, but I stopped him. 'I wonder if you'd mind helping us look. You could search the grounds.'

'If she was out here she'd answer when you called,' he said in a surly voice.

'If she could answer,' I replied.

'I think you ought to come look around,' Elisa said.

Her suggestion carried considerably more weight than mine did. He grunted, but went to get his jacket.

Back in the house I roused a deeply sleeping Miss Wright. She came to her door wrapped in a duster, her mousy hair in curlers. She knew nothing of Maggie's whereabouts either.

'Is there anything you want me to do?' she asked timidly.

'Yes,' I said. 'Make some coffee. I think we're going to need it before this night is over.'

'What are we going to do?' Elisa asked as we came into the hall again.

'Call the police,' I told her, heading for the den with its telephone.

'Is that wise?' she asked, still trailing after me.

'Maggie's missing,' I said, stopping in the doorway. 'It's now almost four in the morning, hardly the time when she would just go out for a stroll. Something has happened. I don't know what, but I intend to find out.'

'But suppose it's something quite innocent,' she argued. 'She'll be furious if she comes home from some personal errand of her own to find we've raised a ruckus. Don't forget, she still has quite a name. A call to the police will bring a horde of reporters descending upon us.'

But I was frightened, in more ways than one. I had been warned that something drastic might happen. I had expected something aimed at me. But had the malice I felt about me been directed instead, for some reason, toward Maggie?

I was frightened, too, because I was alone in the house with Elisa, and Davis was outside, ready at her command. And suddenly, in the darkness of the night, I felt utterly vulnerable.

'I don't think we ought to call the police,' she said, as though her vote decided the matter completely. She took a step toward me. Instinctively I moved backward, away from the doorway. I stepped right into Davis, who had come up behind me silently and without my knowing it. I felt his powerful hands on my arms, holding them in a vice-like grip, and I knew the sensation of panic.

'What's the trouble?' he asked in his coarse voice.

Elisa smiled; it was an expression of malevolent sweetness. 'Nothing, now,' she said. 'We were discussing whether to call the police, but we've decided to postpone that for a while. Isn't that right, Mari?'

I knew I was being delivered a direct challenge. And I knew that, for the moment, I had no means of standing up to it.

'That's right,' I said, looking away from her mocking eyes. The hands holding me relaxed their grip and released me.

12

I moved at once away from both of them, toward the kitchen. Despite my best efforts, I knew they could easily see how shaken I was, and I hated myself for the trembling that had seized me.

'There's just one thing,' I said, facing them squarely despite my fright. 'I want to warn you, if anything has happened to Maggie, I will hold you personally responsible for it.'

Elisa smiled again, but the smile vanished as I added, 'Everything that has happened in this house has been reported to someone else, so threatening me will do you no good either. So don't.'

'I don't know what you mean,' she said in an icy voice. Davis took a step toward me, and I tensed to run, although I could hardly have escaped him. But Elisa raised a hand toward him and he stopped.

'Maggie is my mother,' she said, trying to sound wounded.

'Stepmother,' I corrected her.

'She's been more than a stepmother to me,' she said. 'Would I be up trooping around in the middle of the night if I wasn't worried? I'm the one who woke you up, if you recall, to tell you she was missing.'

'Then you'll have no objection if I call Doctor Wolfe,' I said on an impulse. 'He won't cause any scandal, after all.'

I had expected an argument, but to my surprise she stepped aside without hesitation. 'It might be a good idea if you did,' she said. 'If anything has happened, he might be needed.'

Still expecting some sort of trick, I went warily around her. Neither she nor Davis tried to impede me. I dialed Ken's number, holding my breath until I heard his most welcomed voice.

'Oh, Ken, I'm sorry to bother you, but I need your help. Can you come over right now?'

'Of course,' he said, the sleep disappearing miraculously from his voice. 'What is it?'

'Maggie's missing,' I said, unable to see

from where I stood if Elisa and Davis were still in the hall or if they had gone somewhere else.

'Missing? Have you called the police?'

'No. I'll explain when you get here. Can you come?'

'I'm on my way,' he said. I had nearly hung up the receiver when he said, 'Mari — are you all right?'

'Yes, but hurry,' I said.

Elisa and Davis were nowhere to be seen. I thought of the kitchen and Miss Wright with her coffee, but I did not trust the situation in the house. I went instead to the closet and took out a coat to throw about my shoulders. Then I slipped quietly out the front door, careful to leave it unlocked. I waited there, in the shadows, for Ken to arrive. His headlights swept the driveway very soon. I was in his arms almost before he was out of his car.

'Easy,' he said, holding me close while I cried against his powerful chest. Until this moment I had not realized how completely unnerved I had been.

I told him briefly what had happened. I did not go into detail of how I had been frightened and indirectly threatened by Elisa and Davis. It was over now that he was here; more than that, I was thinking clearly enough now to know that Elisa was right in much of what she had said. A call to the police to report that Maggie Berke was missing would create headlines, headlines Maggie might not appreciate. I explained this to Ken.

'I don't like it,' he said. 'But if you think it's best, we'll sit tight for a little longer.'

'It's nearly morning,' I said. 'Miss Wright was making some coffee, which ought to be ready by now. If Maggie hasn't come home by, say, nine o'clock, then we can contact the authorities. Let's give her that long.'

'Okay,' he said, leading me toward the house again. 'But I'm still not fully convinced.'

If Elisa was unhappy to see Ken she concealed the fact quite well. Had I not known better, I would almost have thought she genuinely welcomed his presence. Davis was nowhere to be seen, and Miss Wright had fled at the sound of Ken's voice to the safety of her own room.

Ken questioned Elisa, but she had little to add to what I had already told him. She had accompanied Maggie upstairs at about eleven. She did not know whether Maggie had taken the sleeping pills she sometimes used, strong ones prescribed by Ken himself. So far as she knew, Maggie had intended nothing more than going to bed and sleeping the night away.

'No sign of an intruder?' Ken asked both of us.

'Not that I could see,' I answered, and Elisa nodded her agreement.

He sighed and helped himself to a second cup of coffee. 'That certainly makes it look like she left under her own power,' he said.

'But why?' I asked. 'And for where?'

He cocked an eyebrow. 'You know, she's not a baby. Has it occurred to you, for instance, that she is still a reasonably attractive woman?'

I blushed at the implication in his question. More than that, it sounded as if he were siding with Elisa. But he hadn't been here when Elisa had delivered her faintly veiled threats, nor when Davis's strong hands had held me in check when I wanted to telephone the police. I said nothing of these things, but my heart felt leaden within me.

We sat disconsolately about the kitchen, sipping coffee and glancing frequently at the clock. It seemed to be hours longer than it actually was. As nine approached, Ken again voiced his opinion that we ought to summon the authorities. I still hesitated, and Elisa faintly sided with me. We compromised, agreeing to wait another half hour.

Before that time was up, Maggie was home.

As it was, she returned in the company of a deputy sheriff, and she looked as if she had been out for anything but a rendezvous. Her hair was uncombed and straggly, the remnants of her makeup smeared hideously. Her clothes were wrinkled and dirty. She looked pathetic.

'Maggie!' I exclaimed when I answered the door to find her there. 'What on earth has happened? Where have you been? We've been worried sick.'

She wore a dazed expression. I realized suddenly how fully exhausted she was, and I took her into my arms. 'No, never mind, don't try to explain now,' I said. 'You look all in.'

'I think she is,' the deputy said, following us into the hall. 'Somebody better get her to bed.'

'I'll see to that,' Elisa said, taking charge of Maggie.

I let her escort Maggie up the stairs. When they were around the curve in the staircase, I turned back to the deputy, who had waited. 'Where did you find her?' I asked.

'She was wandering around in the Arthur Field Cemetery,' he said grimly, shaking his head. 'The caretaker saw her and called us. She didn't know how she had gotten there, or even where she was. She seemed . . . well, I hate to say it, but weird, like she wasn't quite right upstairs, you know what I mean?' He paused for a moment. 'She knew who she was all right. When I heard her name, I almost flipped. I'm an old movie fan. I've watched Maggie Berke maybe a hundred times on the tube. What I'm trying to say is, I should have taken her down to the station and gone through all the formalities. But I figured if I did that, there'd be one hell of a stink, with the reporters and all. And I just didn't have the heart to do that to her. So I brought her back here instead.'

'I'm grateful to you,' I said sincerely. 'And I know Maggie will be too, when she's feeling better.'

He grinned ruefully. 'Yeah. I hope she is soon. But I better warn you, if she does this sort of thing regularly, you're gonna have problems. The next cop may not be a movie buff, you know what I mean?'

'She doesn't do it regularly,' I said. I could not say more without venturing into a subject I did not want to discuss with this man. 'I do wish you'd leave me your name,' I said instead. 'I know Maggie will want to thank you herself. As long as you're a movie fan, perhaps she could share some of her memories with you.'

He was pleased with the suggestion, and wrote his name and address in Maggie's notebook for me. When he had gone, Ken suggested he ought to take a look at Maggie.

'I want to know what was behind this,' he said, taking his bag upstairs with him.

I waited in the kitchen, where Miss Wright, dressed now and wearing a disapproving expression, was busy fixing breakfast. Ken and Elisa came down together a short time later.

'She's all right,' Ken assured me. 'Physically exhausted and chilled from being out in the night like that, but otherwise all right. I'll come back this afternoon for another look, but for now I think the best thing for her is some sound sleep.'

'I'm grateful that you were here,' Elisa told him, 'so that you could see for yourself how her faculties have deteriorated. I don't want anyone thinking I'm exaggerating the state of Maggie's mind.'

I suddenly understood why Elisa had not resisted my announced intention of phoning Ken. 'I don't know that anything has been proven,' I said uneasily.

Elisa raised her eyebrows. 'I hope you don't consider this the act of a rational person,' she said. 'Disappearing in the middle of the night, wandering around in cemeteries at dawn, unable even to remember where she is? How would you regard it, Doctor Wolfe?'

'I'm not entirely sure,' he said. He turned to me instead. 'I've got to go.'

'I'll walk to your car with you,' I said.

'Think how this would sound to another doctor,' Elisa said as we started from the room. 'One not quite so reluctant to face the facts of the case.'

'It won't be necessary to call in another doctor,' Ken said.

'I hope not,' was her reply.

13

Outside, I asked Ken the question that had been on my mind since Maggie's return. 'Ken, what happened to her?'

'I don't know,' he said frankly.

'Could she have been drugged?'

He sighed and shook his head. 'Possibly,' he said. 'There's some evidence of drugs. But Maggie keeps some pretty powerful pills around the place — sleeping pills, tranquilizers, sedatives. I've tried to discourage her from using them, but she still occasionally loads herself up with them. It's possible she might have gotten pilled up and wandered away by herself, without remembering much about it afterward. If she did . . . well, as Elisa says, it isn't a very healthy sign.'

'But if she didn't?' I said. 'Isn't it just as possible that someone maybe took her out? Suppose Elisa pumped her full of pills? Maggie was upset last night, and Elisa did give her some pills. Suppose afterward, when Maggie was really out cold, Elisa dressed Maggie and drove her to that cemetery and left her to wake up and find herself there. She could have driven back to the house after that, and come to my room to announce that Maggie was missing.'

'But why?'

'So that you could see Maggie behaving strangely,' I said. 'So that, if need be, she could call in another doctor, provide all kinds of witnesses — you, me, Miss Wright, that sheriff, Davis — all to testify to Maggie's eccentricity.'

'Maybe,' he said. 'But it's a pretty tough charge to make stick. We don't have anything but suspicion on our side.'

He kissed me lightly and got into his car. I watched him drive out of sight before turning back to the house. Its windows seemed to watch me. I felt an urge to turn about and run away from this increasingly disturbing atmosphere. But I could not. Whatever threatened me, I had to face up to it. And whatever Elisa's motives or methods, I had one weapon on my side that she lacked: I was in the right.

Maggie slept through most of the day. Late in the afternoon she rang for Miss Wright and asked for something to eat. I had been listening for the summons and when Miss Wright had prepared some hot broth, I took it up to Maggie's room myself. I wanted to hear the story of Maggie's misadventure from Maggie herself.

As it turned out, she could add nothing to the story I had already gotten from the deputy sheriff who brought her home.

'I wish I could tell you what happened,' she said wearily, 'but I just don't remember. I know that Elisa came upstairs with me and saw me to my room. I don't think she came in with me, but from that point on my memory fails me. The next thing I knew, I was in a strange place. I realized it was a cemetery, and it was morning, but where I was or how I had come to be there I have no idea.'

'Maggie, when Elisa brought you up, did she give you any pills or medicine?' I asked.

She shook her head. 'I don't remember. Wait. Yes, she brought my tranquilizers downstairs to me before that. I was upset.'

'How many pills did you take?'

'I don't know. But Elisa gave them to me, and she would have taken care to see that I didn't take more than prescribed. She's very careful about those things.'

I did not share her confidence in Elisa, but she looked so forlorn that I didn't have the heart to pursue the subject any further. When she had finished eating, I took the tray away and she announced her intention of sleeping again.

I came back to her room later, however, when I was confident Maggie would be asleep. I knocked first at the door; when there was no answer I let myself into the room. Maggie was deep in slumber in the dimly lit room.

I meant to examine the clothes she had been wearing in the morning. It occurred to me that they might offer some clue. But they were nowhere to be found. I checked everything in the laundry hamper but there was no trace of that particular outfit. It seemed to have disappeared.

When I came back downstairs I went to

the kitchen, where I found Miss Wright, and asked her about them, but she knew nothing of the missing clothes. 'I suppose they went into the laundry,' was all she could offer. 'I'll look for them, if you like.'

'No, that won't be necessary,' I said. 'It wasn't of any importance; I was just curious.'

I felt confident that she would not find the clothes. They were gone, I was sure of that, and I thought I knew why. It was not the sort of outfit Maggie would have chosen for herself, even when not thinking clearly. Maggie had lived a life of glamor for so long that by now an act such as choosing an attractive and suitable outfit was nearly instinctive. She might, under the influence of drugs, overlook wrinkles and such, perhaps even color. But I doubted that Maggie would have picked an extremely outdated, now ill-fitting outfit such as the one she had worn. Nor would she have put on a pair of forty-ish walking slippers. Her entire costume for her night-time sojourn had been made up of 'slip-ons' — clothes and shoes that one person could put on another with a minimum of effort. And clothes that might easily be selected by someone with Elisa's lack of taste.

I was convinced that Maggie had been taken from the house after being drugged and dressed, but I had no evidence that would carry any weight. I needed some proof positive of the grimly serious game Elisa was playing with her stepmother. I was the only thing that stood between Maggie and the success of Elisa's scheme, and I meant to remain there as long as necessary.

Elisa was far from done with me, however. In my renewed concern for Maggie I had almost forgotten that Elisa's malevolence was directed against me as well. I was reminded of that fact the very same night.

The previous night's interrupted sleep had left me more than ordinarily tired, and I went to bed early, falling almost at once into a deep, exhausted sleep.

I did not know exactly what awakened me. I had an impression that something had brushed my face softly, like the gentle stroking of a hand.

I did awaken, however, and in that brief moment before I opened my eyes, I knew at once that I was not alone in the room. Someone was with me.

I opened my eyes and sat up as I did so. In the darkness I could only just make out the figure in white that moved silently away from the bed, toward the open door. Even before I had time to cry 'Wait,' the ghostly figure had disappeared into the hall.

My fear was brief, replaced almost at once by anger. This was no ghost, but an all-too-solid human being, dressed in billowing white, come to frighten me.

'Wait,' I cried again, jumping from my bed to race across the room. But my moment of hesitation had given my visitor time to escape. I had a glimpse of white disappearing down the stairs.

I had a good idea who my 'ghost' was and I meant to prove my point before she could get back to her room. I went directly to the door of Elisa's room. I knocked loudly and then, without waiting, I threw open the door.

To my astonishment, she was in bed, in her nightgown. She sat up as the door opened, giving me a wide-eyed look, and clutching the covers before her.

There was no way that the figure who ran down the stairs could have gotten back into the room so quickly.

'What on earth?' Elisa said.

'Something was in my room,' I said lamely. 'Or someone.'

'Well, you can see for yourself it wasn't me,' she said indignantly.

'Well it was certainly no ghost,' I said. 'It was someone in this house.'

She smiled tolerantly, as one might to a stubborn child. 'That hardly seems likely,' she said. 'Unless you think it was Miss Wright. Or Maggie?'

I felt increasingly foolish. Miss Wright, bland creature that she was, was hardly likely to take part in any bogus haunting; and of course it wasn't Maggie. Nor could that frail, fleet figure have been Davis.

'I'm sorry I disturbed you,' I said, knowing that my humiliation was apparent. I turned to leave.

'You were warned, you know,' Elisa said behind me. 'The spirits warned you that you were in danger here. Perhaps you ought to take their advice and leave.'

I looked back at her, my eyes blazing. 'I'm not afraid,' I told her. 'And you can tell your spirits that.'

This was not quite the truth. I *was* frightened, because I did not know what Elisa would try next, or how I could thwart her. All that I knew for certain was that she would try again. She meant to have Maggie put out of this house and into an institution. And to accomplish that goal, she meant to drive me from this place as well.

14

Looking back on those uncertain days, I realize that I compounded my difficulties with my indecision. In part this was because I knew so little of what I was combating. I knew that Elisa planned to have Maggie put away, but I did not understand quite why. I felt confident that the 'haunting' of the house was managed by Elisa, but again I did not know how. I felt that I must expose her and defeat her plan, but I did not know by what means. I was sparring with shadows — phantoms — as ghostly as those that Maggie believed wandered the halls of The Aerie.

I woke the following morning faced with another troublesome decision. Should I tell Maggie of the ghostly visitor to my room? I knew it would only add to her unhappiness. On the other hand, I wanted to make her understand that these incidents were being caused by all-too-human individuals whose purpose was to frighten me away and drive her mad.

In the end, I concluded that Maggie would be unlikely to believe my version of events, and I did not care to contribute to her belief in ghosts. When I saw her that morning, I made no mention of the strange visitor that had disturbed my sleep.

If I thought, however, that by keeping this story to myself I would ensure that Maggie was undisturbed, I was mistaken. When I went to see her, soon after she had breakfasted in bed, she was obviously upset.

'Maggie,' I said, looking at the scarcely disarranged tray. 'You've hardly eaten a thing.'

'I'm afraid I haven't much appetite,' she said, making a face at the eggs Florentine Miss Wright had prepared with obvious care. She was becoming agitated again. 'Oh, Mari, what if I've only imagined all these spirits? If it were just the one incident, it would be different, but it isn't. You don't know what it's like, not knowing if . . . ' Her voice broke and she began to cry, covering her face with her hands. She looked so pathetic that I went at once to her side, sitting on the edge of the bed and taking her in my arms.

'Darling Mari,' she said through her sobbing. 'I do love you. You believe that, don't you?'

'Of course I do,' I assured her.

'And you'll believe that, no matter what happens, won't you? Even if something terrible happens, even if I seem to be . . . not right? Please believe that I don't want to hurt you.' She was speaking rapidly, almost incoherently. Her sobbing became more hysterical. I tried to comfort her but she seemed scarcely to hear me. 'I don't want to hurt you,' she said over and over. 'I never want to harm you.'

There were tranquilizers on the nightstand. Ken had assured me that these were mild and safe, and I persuaded Maggie to take one with some water. After a time, she grew calm again, but she was far from being herself.

'I'm so tired,' she mumbled, sinking into the pillow. 'I sleep so much, and still I'm tired.'

'You've exhausted yourself,' I said, patting her shoulder comfortingly. 'Why don't you get some more rest, and I'll come back to see you again later?'

She fixed her gaze upon me, studying me in a strange way as if etching my likeness on her consciousness. 'Has something happened?' I asked on an impulse.

'No,' she said quickly — too quickly, I thought. But I did not risk disturbing her again by pursuing the subject. I kissed her forehead and went out of the room.

Something had happened to disturb Maggie, I was convinced of that — something beyond the escapade with the cemetery. Whatever it was had frightened her, and it concerned my safety. Again and again she had repeated that she did not want to harm me. I recalled that there had been several warnings regarding my safety. Perhaps, I thought, she was feeling guilty for letting me stay, assuming a responsibility for some dire fate she feared would fall upon me.

I met Ken for lunch and brought him up to date on the events of the night. Of course he was disturbed to know that a new attempt had been made to intimidate me.

'I don't like this,' he said. 'I think you had better move out of the house. Let me find you a hotel room.'

'But if I did that,' I said, 'there'd be no one there to watch out for Maggie.'

'You could get a room nearby, and spend your days at the house with Maggie.'

'And leave her alone at night? No. I've even given thought to moving a bed into her room, except she'd think I was going crazy too, and Elisa would never stand still for it anyway. But I feel that I am needed there, Ken. If I moved out now I would feel like I'm deserting Maggie.'

'I still don't like it,' he said, unconvinced. 'And there's this new business of Maggie's being afraid she'll hurt you.'

'I promise you I'll be extra careful.'

'Let's compromise,' he said. 'You'll go on staying at the house so long as nothing further happens. But one more of these mysterious happenings and out you go to a hotel room.'

'We'll see,' I said. I didn't want to promise. Still, I hoped there would be no more mysterious happenings.

'What about Maggie's sanity?' I asked

later in the meal. 'What's necessary to have a person committed?'

'Surprisingly enough it's not all that difficult,' he said. He paused while the waiter cleared away our dishes and brought coffee. 'Basically, all that's required is that a doctor testify to the patient's condition,' he went on. 'There may be a hearing or there may not be. Normally, as Maggie's regular doctor, I would be the one to testify. But any doctor can do that if called in by the family.'

'Then Elisa could make good her threat to have Maggie committed even if you refused to testify to her insanity?'

'Unfortunately, yes,' he said.

'Do you think another doctor would testify to it?'

He nodded sadly. 'Unfortunately, yes, considering the recent developments.'

I sighed and gave my attention to the dessert tray the waiter had brought. In this game, Elisa already held all the high cards. Somehow, I had to find some way of trumping them before the game was over.

I had promised Ken to take extra care,

but it did not occur to me that the ghostly visit to my room might become a regular affair. If it had, I would certainly have taken precautions such as locking my door, or even leaving a light on to get a better look. As it was, I did none of these when I went to bed that night.

When I was awakened, I knew at once what it was. I sat up immediately, eyes flying open. This time she was at the door, which was open. She had opened it loudly, flinging it back against the wall with a bang, and it was this that had roused me. From the distance across the room, she did indeed look ghostlike, a figure in billowy white, her outlines blurred in the darkness. She stood framed in the doorway, one hand summoning me.

All right, I thought, *I'll play your silly game.* I clambered from the high bed. As I did so, my visitor turned and disappeared into the hallway.

I went quickly after her. By the time I reached the door, she was already well down the hall, toward the sweeping stairs that led down to the first floor. She paused, looking back to be sure that I was after her. Then she glided lightly down the stairs.

At the head of the stairs I paused too. She was at the first floor already. Where was she leading me, and why? Was there some sort of trap set for me? Was I walking into danger?

I had not come completely unprepared, however. In my purse I carried a pocket-sized flashlight, and I had thought to bring this with me as I came from my room. I had thought to save it as a surprise when a propitious moment presented itself. But as I started down the dark stairs, answering the silent summons of the white figure below, I flicked on the tiny light, aiming it in front of my feet.

A glimmer of light sprang back up at me. I realized its significance too late to avoid tripping over the thin wire that had been stretched across the stairs, but that split second of warning saved me from a broken leg, maybe even a broken neck.

As I toppled forward I made a grab for the stair rail. My fingers slipped from its polished surface, but the grab had broken my fall. I slid down a couple of steps and managed on the second try to grab the banister. My flashlight rolled and banged on its way down the stairs, the light disappearing somewhere along the way.

15

I sat for several moments in stunned silence, scarcely comprehending what had happened. I heard scuffling above me and realized that I must have screamed as I fell. A light came on in the hall and a moment later Elisa appeared at the top of the stairs.

'What's happened?' she asked, staring down at me.

'Wait there just a moment,' I snapped. I scrambled angrily to my feet. I felt a little bruised and sore, but otherwise sound. And I was as mad as the proverbial wet hen. Someone had deliberately set a trap for me and lured me into it, a trap that might have cost me my life. And I wanted to know who that someone was.

I went down the rest of the stairs quickly but cautiously, holding tightly onto the banister in case another trap had been set somewhere. On the way I stopped to retrieve my flashlight where it had landed. It was no longer working.

Of course by this time my figure in white had managed to disappear. There was no trace of her. I went from room to room turning on lights, but she had vanished. I told myself that my search was futile. She had had more than ample time to hide herself, or even to leave the house.

When I came back into the hall, both Elisa and Maggie were there, Maggie looking frightened in her pale, fluffy gown. 'What is it?' she asked. 'What's happened this time? What are you looking for?'

'Someone who set a booby trap for me on the stairs,' I replied, giving Elisa a hard look.

'A booby trap?' Maggie glanced in the direction of the stairs.

'A piece of wire,' I said. 'Stretched across the stairs so that I would trip over it. And a visitor in ghostly white robes beckoning me out of my room and down the stairs, so that I could trip and break my neck.'

'I didn't see any wire,' Elisa said.

'Nor I,' Maggie agreed.

'Did you remove it, dear? It's a wonder

one of us didn't trip too.'

'No, it's still . . . ' But before I had finished the sentence I had an inkling of what had happened. I went up the stairs two at a time. But of course, there was no wire there now and no evidence to prove that there ever had been a wire stretched across the stairs.

Elisa and Maggie came up the stairs more slowly, Maggie looking puzzled, Elisa looking, I thought, smug.

'There was a wire here,' I said stubbornly, pointing at the steps. 'Right about here. I saw it. And I certainly tripped over it.'

'The carpet is a little loose in spots,' Elisa said calmly. 'Perhaps you caught your foot somewhere and lost your balance. It could seem like you had tripped over a wire, perhaps.'

'There was a wire,' I insisted.

'But there's none there now,' Maggie said, looking up and down the stairs.

'Someone dressed up like a ghost has been trying to frighten me,' I argued. 'Tonight it lured me out of my room, and I tripped over a wire.'

'Or you dreamed the whole thing,' Elisa suggested in a gentle, patronizing tone.

I returned her gaze angrily. I knew that she had outwitted me again. It would have taken no more than a few seconds for her to remove the wire while I went on down the stairs in search of her accomplice. And she would have had ample time to do it before Maggie reached the stairs from her room further down the hall. Perhaps, I thought, furious with myself for having given her such a gratuitous opportunity, she meant to prove me insane too.

When I returned to my room this time, I took the precaution of locking my door. I did not care for any repeat visits from my eerie friend, not tonight at least.

In the morning I had several colorful bruises to remind me of my midnight adventure. Fortunately none of them were where they would be conspicuous.

I had decided against telling Ken what had happened. While I disliked even a lie of omission where he was concerned, I knew that he would insist upon my moving out of the house if he knew, and I was not yet ready to do that. I had a feeling that things were moving toward some sort of climax, and I wanted to be on hand here when it occurred. Elisa's moves were getting more and more violent, suggesting that she was getting increasingly desperate. And the more desperate one's opponent becomes, the greater are his chances of making an error.

As it turned out, Ken was not the only person who felt I should move. It seemed, in fact, as if everyone concerned wanted me out of the house. To my surprise, Maggie once again changed her mind on the subject. She came to me in the morning with the announcement that she had decided I should go.

'I've come to the conclusion that it really isn't safe here for you,' she explained. We were in my room, where I was finishing dressing for the day. Although she still looked drawn and pale, she seemed to have recovered from her own unpleasant experience. She was out of bed, dressed elegantly in a black silk dress that heightened her faded appearance and made her look all the more melancholy.

'This business on the stairs last night?'

I asked. 'That won't happen again, I assure you. I mean to keep my door locked at night in the future.'

'It's not just that,' she said. 'There were all the warnings, if you recall.'

'But we aren't sure they came from Buddy,' I reminded her, falling back upon her own belief in the ghosts that supposedly haunted the place.

She shrugged off my arguments. 'Regardless of who wants you gone, Buddy or some other poor soul, the fact is you are in danger. The chandelier suggested it, but because I wanted your company in the house, I was willing to accept that as an accident. Last night, however, was too much of a coincidence. Even I must admit that.'

'That was no spirit last night,' I said. 'It was someone very much human.'

'I can't imagine why,' she said. 'Why would anyone want to dress up like a ghost? Why would a real person want to harm you?'

I hesitated, trying to decide how much of what I had to tell her Maggie would be able to accept.

'Suppose I said I don't believe there are any ghosts here at all?' I said finally. 'What if all the things that have been happening have been perpetrated by human beings?'

'Why, that makes no sense,' she said, looking bewildered. 'I've talked to Buddy myself. He's given me messages.'

'During Madame Davina's séances?' I asked.

'Yes, but not only there. I've seen him. Oh, not face to face, I'll admit that. And if it were only a ghostly figure at a distance, I would be willing to grant it might be an imposter. But I've heard his voice, calling me.'

I knew that she was becoming upset again, and I felt her slipping away from me. But I had to make one more try. 'That could be a recording,' I said. 'Or a good impersonator.'

'I don't believe that,' she said, shaking her head. 'I know Buddy's voice. And how could they do a recording without Buddy? No, he has come back.'

I seized Maggie's hands in mine, determined to make her see the truth.

'What did he say to you?'

'Oh, all kinds of things,' she said, biting at her lip. 'Once he said, 'Mother, mother, how could you?' and then he began to cry. Don't you see? It's because I failed him, because I let him die while I was out partying and carrying on.'

'That's nonsense,' I said, releasing her hands.

She sighed deeply and sat down in the chair at my dressing table. 'There's something else,' she said. 'Something that couldn't have been faked. You see, Buddy has come to me in my dreams too.'

'That's reasonable,' I said. 'You have him on your mind a great deal of the time; too much of the time, in fact. It's only logical that you would dream of him.'

'But these aren't ordinary dreams. The things he says to me in my dreams confirm what the voices I hear tell me. Sometimes they clarify something, or vice versa. And I've never discussed my dreams with anyone. So it couldn't be just coincidence, you see. If it were only the physical manifestations, I might think they were somehow faked. I even

181

suspected that at first, at the very beginning. I'm not a completely stupid woman, don't you understand? But the dreams were real, and explicit. He's given me instructions in them; for instance, where to find certain things. And when I looked, there they were. He's told me things that I would hear in an upcoming séance, and I've heard them. Even if Madame Divina were the world's greatest fake, she couldn't know what I had been told in my dreams.'

I was dumbfounded. I had no argument for this. 'There must be an explanation,' I said, but my voice did not sound convincing even to my own ears.

She gave me a sympathetic smile. 'I know how you feel at this moment,' she said. 'It is crazy, isn't it? It made no sense to me either, until I accepted the most logical explanation. Buddy has come back to me.'

I started to speak but she motioned me to silence. 'There's more,' she said. 'I hadn't meant to tell you, but I see now that I must, in order to make you understand my position . . . and yours. I pray that it will not turn you against me, but I see I must take that risk.'

'I'm certain it won't,' I said.

'The last few nights, Buddy has come to me again in my dreams.'

'And,' I said, guessing what she was going to tell me, 'he says I have to leave.'

'Not at all,' she said. 'He has told me that I must take your life!'

I stared at her in shocked silence, unable to believe what I had heard.

'He says,' she repeated, 'that I must kill you. So, you see, for both our sakes, I must make you leave this house.'

16

There was nothing for me to do but agree to Maggie's insistence that I leave. I still did not believe in her 'ghosts', but I was more in the dark than ever about how to convince her that they were not real. To have stayed on would have been to cause her a great deal of anguish, and expose myself to danger.

There was a nice hotel only a short distance away on the Strip and I was lucky enough to get very pleasant rooms there.

'It's quite charming,' Maggie said when we looked over the rooms. She had insisted on paying for a suite for me and coming with me to be sure that it was good enough.

It was, in all fairness, a lovely suite, furnished with tasteful modern pieces, and with a view nearly as grand as that from Maggie's house. I had only to step out of the lobby to be caught up in all the whirlwind activity of the Strip. Still, I could not help feeling more than a little dejected.

'I suppose the sensible thing to do would have been to return to Minneapolis,' I said.

'And cramp your romance with the handsome Doctor Wolfe?' she asked with a twinkle in her eye.

'But Maggie, I can't go on forever living out of a hotel suite.'

'Of course not. But a few weeks won't hurt a thing. And who knows, maybe Buddy will give me a new message now that we've done what he wanted and moved you out. I see now that I've been foolish. I should have listened to my voices from the beginning and avoided all this trouble.'

There seemed to be nothing I could say in answer to this, and I directed my attention instead to putting away some of my things.

Having seen that I was comfortably ensconced, Maggie departed, promising she would call me a dozen times every day to let me know how she was. Despite her promises, however, I felt certain that, with me out of the house, things would grow even worse for her.

I told Ken this later. He of course was delighted that I had moved into the hotel. He came by later that day for cocktails.

'At least I don't have to worry about someone carrying you off in the night,' he said over his martini. 'Or locking you up in the dungeon of that place.'

'No, now it's Maggie who will be carried away, or locked up in the dungeon,' I said dispiritedly.

'Maybe,' he said. 'But remember this. We know that they're up to something, and they know we know it. They might decide to play it cool for a while. And that might give us time to sort things out.'

'If only I understood how they can manipulate her dreams,' I said. I had already told him of the voices that spoke to her in her sleep, and of the grim message they had delivered regarding me.

He was thoughtful for a moment. 'It might be some sort of hypnosis,' he said.

'That's not exactly my field, but I might investigate that possibility. I'll call a few colleagues tomorrow and see if they have any ideas.' He set aside his drink and came around to where I was sitting, lifting me out of the chair and into his arms. 'But for now, you're going to forget all about the pack of them. This, your first night out of that house, is going to be nothing but romance, all right?'

That was one order I didn't mind obeying.

* * *

After my night of romance, however, I was eager to get back to the question of Maggie's haunting. Ken had promised again to check into the possibilities of hypnosis influencing Maggie's dreams. And I had a few ideas of my own that I wanted to look into. By nine thirty the following morning, having assured myself on the phone that Maggie had spent a perfectly excitement-free evening, I was in the office of Sam Carr, Maggie's former agent and long-time friend.

'Remember you?' he said when I was ushered into his luxurious office overlooking most of downtown Hollywood. 'I've thought of nobody else since I first set eyes on you.'

His bantering tone was a welcome change from the atmosphere in which I had been living for several days. 'I'm sure you must say that to a hundred different girls a day,' I replied, accepting the chair he offered me.

'No more than a dozen,' he corrected me, grinning. 'But I know what brings most of them here. What brings you? Decided you wanted to try acting anyway?'

'No, but I have come for a favor. Not just for myself, though. It's for Maggie.'

He grew sober at once. 'How is she?'

'Not very well, I'm afraid,' I said.

He sighed and lit a big cigar from the gold box on his desk. 'I know something's been wrong up there. It has been for a long time, but she's never confided in me about it, and I learned a long time ago that with Maggie it didn't pay to pry.'

'It isn't really my story to tell,' I said, choosing my words carefully. 'Although I'm sure in time you'll hear all of it. But for now, I'll have to ask you to trust me, and believe that I'm trying to help Maggie.'

'What's your favor?' he asked.

He was a little surprised by my request, but he respected my reasons for not explaining any more fully. 'Will it be possible?' I asked when I had told him what I wanted.

'Downright simple,' he assured me. He made a brief phone call. That completed, he instructed his secretary to have his car brought around. 'Let's go,' he said to me.

Doors seemed to open like magic before Sam Carr — the doors to his limousine, the gates to Horizon Films, and the doors to the offices of Sid Whalen, the studio head. Mr. Whalen insisted he remembered meeting me, although I was certain he did not, and I was thankful I had decided to go to Sam rather than directly to the big man. Maggie might still be a legend, but to most people her niece was still a nobody.

'Don't know why anyone would want to spend a whole day looking at them,' Whalen said as he ushered us into the studio's big projection room. 'But the films are all ready. Got my own private projectionist in the booth. You just give him any instructions you have.' With that he left Sam and me alone in the projection room.

By the time I had viewed two of Buddy Berke's old films my spirits were flagging. I had begun to think I was on a wild goose chase when Buddy's now familiar voice said from the screen, 'Mother, mother.'

I leaned tensely forward, but the words that followed were not the ones I wanted to hear. It was not until a few minutes later when the child star was crying loudly in one scene that another possibility occurred to me.

'Would it be possible,' I asked Sam Carr, 'to put together excerpts from several films? Just the voice parts, I mean.'

'On tape?'

'Yes, I suppose it would be on tape. So that Buddy would be saying something he never actually said in one of his movies. A sentence or a phrase made up out of words he had said in different films.'

'Sure, with a good recorder and prints of the films. Nothing but an editing job.'

'Does Maggie have these films?'

He chuckled. 'Every one of them, and every one of her own, as well. Locked up in a big room in the basement. She used to show them a lot, but not in the last ten, fifteen years. I guess she and Elisa must know every line in every one of these films.'

'But if the words were rearranged,' I said, as much to myself as to him, 'into a different message, Maggie wouldn't associate them — wouldn't recognize them as coming from any particular one of his movies. And you would have a Buddy Berke recording without the necessity of Buddy actually being there.'

'Simplest thing in the world to do,' he said. He was studying me carefully and I felt he had begun to suspect what I was getting at, but he maintained a tactful silence on that score. I told him what I was seeking. He nodded and grinned, and spoke briefly to the projectionist.

Five minutes later, Buddy Berke was on the screen again, in a different movie, and I was listening to him ask a youthful playmate: 'How could you?'

17

Ken was no less excited than I was when we met for cocktails in the hotel lounge. He listened with scarcely concealed impatience as I explained about the movie dialogue.

'They've taken words and phrases from a variety of his films,' I concluded, 'and put them together on tapes to provide new messages, virtually anything they wanted his so-called ghost to say to Maggie.'

'And of course, with the way they were even making her dreams talk to her, it took little convincing to make her believe the messages were authentic,' he agreed. 'As for the dreams, I spent the day learning how that could be done — and incidentally, how they managed a few other things,' he said. 'It was hypnosis of a sort. The key is that a hypnotist can put a subject who is already asleep into a hypnotic trance by speaking to him while he's asleep. Ideally, it should be a voice that the subject knows and trusts. The hypnotist starts by ordering the subject not to wake up, but to go into a deeper sleep. Then he talks the subject into a hypnotic trance and can give him virtually any instructions he wants. In this way a good hypnotist can even bring about a trance in a subject who otherwise can't be hypnotized.'

'Then all Elisa had to do,' I said, sharing his excitement, 'was tell her she was hearing Buddy's voice, and give her whatever message they wanted.'

'Right. Or tell her that the figure she saw moving around in the house was Buddy, and she'd believe it. Or tell her to get up, help get herself dressed in the clothes they had laid out for her, drive her to a cemetery, and leave her to find herself there in the morning — with instructions that she would remember none of it when she woke up.'

'That's it,' I said. 'That must be how it was done.'

'Just one catch,' he said, frowning. 'The knowledge doesn't do us much good. We can't go to the police. Except for giving you a rough time, there's no particular crime they've committed. And we'll never convince Maggie so long as they can go right on muddying her thinking with their 'messages'. She's no doubt under a strong hypnotic suggestion to believe them.'

'But there is one thing we can do,' I said. 'All we really need is to get Maggie away from Elisa for a few days; just long enough for her to collect her wits, right?'

'Yes, probably. A few days without repeated suggestions, and someone telling her the truth instead.'

'You're her doctor,' I said. 'Order her to take a trip. Prescribe it for her nerves. A few days out of town — say Hawaii — ought to do wonders.'

'Especially,' he said, grinning, 'with you as her companion.'

'I wouldn't put it quite that way. Arrange for a nurse to accompany her. That way Elisa can't object, and there's no legitimate reason for her to come along. Of course, we don't have to tell them that I'm going to be the nurse.'

'It might work,' he agreed. 'At least, it's worth a try.'

As we expected, Maggie was reluctant at first, but I had gone to the house with Ken, and between the two of us we were able to persuade her that he was right. By the time we left, she had actually begun to show some enthusiasm for the idea.

'Imagine, a trip,' she said as she saw us out. 'I haven't gone anywhere in decades. Oh Mari, how I wish you were coming with me.'

'Who knows,' I said, suppressing a smile. 'I'm on the loose. I might even decide to join you in Hawaii.'

I disliked deceiving Maggie, but under the circumstances I felt it was justified. I was certain that if Elisa knew I was joining Maggie, she would manage somehow to prevent Maggie's going.

Having agreed to the trip, Maggie had offered no objections to going at once. We had agreed that I would pick her up the following evening to take her to the airport. I spent most of the next day rushing about, picking up items I thought I would need. It was late in the afternoon when I returned to my hotel room to pack. To my surprise, there was a message for me, from Maggie. It said, simply, that she would not be able to keep our appointment.

I tried calling the house. I got a recording telling me that the telephone had been temporarily disconnected, at the request of the subscriber.

For a moment I sat in my room, staring at the telephone and contemplating this change of events. I was certain the message came not from Maggie but from Elisa. Perhaps she had suspected the purpose of the trip; or perhaps she simply did not care to let Maggie out of her sight at this point in her venture. But what exactly could I do?

I put in a call to Ken at his office, but he had already gone. He had planned to make several calls and then to meet Maggie and me at the airport.

'It's important I reach Doctor Wolfe,' I explained to the woman at his exchange. 'Is there any way I can get in touch with him?'

'I can try to call him on his cell phone and give him your message,' she informed me.

'Couldn't you give me the number and let me try to reach him?' I asked.

'I'm sorry,' was her clipped reply, 'but we're not permitted to do that without special instructions from Doctor Wolfe.'

I fought down my frustration; she was only following orders. I left my name and number and hung up despondently. The sun was setting. The sky had taken on a pearlescent tone; the clouds were pink and gray and bordered in gold.

I had a sudden sense of urgency. Call it premonition, intuition, whatever you will. I suddenly did not feel that I could wait for Ken to call. I knew with certainty that Maggie needed me now. I left a message at the desk, saying that I had gone to The Aerie. In a few minutes I was in a cab, speeding up the Strip.

How ominous that house looked as the cab came up the familiar curving drive. When it had come to a stop, I sat for a moment, staring at the unfriendly door.

'This is the right place, ain't it, miss?' the driver asked.

'Yes, this is it,' I said, shaking off my lethargy. I paid him and alighted from the vehicle. I would have liked to have asked him to wait, so that I could bring Maggie straight out, and be away from here without any delays. But there was no telling what I might encounter inside.

'Want me to wait?' he asked.

'No, thank you,' I said, and turned to the house. When I heard him start off, I glanced back at him. If I had given in to impulse, I would have run after him, gone back to the hotel, and waited for Ken. But I knew I could not do that.

Instead, I made myself mount the steps to the front door. The dragon's head knocker seemed to gleam wickedly. How long ago it seemed since I had first lifted it and heard its echo inside, and how different this occasion was. Even the knocking that sounded within seemed changed. Then it had been a pleasant sound. Now it seemed to me a grim knell.

There was no reply. I waited for a long pause. Then I lifted the knocker again and rapped more loudly. There was another long silence. Then, just as I was reaching for the dragon's head to knock again, the door opened with such abruptness that I jumped. Elisa stood framed in the doorway, regarding me with undisguised coldness.

'What is it?' she asked.

'I've come to see Maggie,' I said. I would have gone on inside but she stood directly in the way, blocking the entrance to the house.

'I believe she sent you a message,' Elisa said. 'At your hotel.'

'I received it,' I said. 'But I want to see Maggie and talk to her myself.'

'That won't be possible,' she said. She made a move as though to close the door, but I stepped forward and blocked it with my foot.

'Why not?'

'She's asleep,' she said. 'She left instructions that she was not to be disturbed.'

'I don't believe you,' I said. I was tired of this sparring. 'And I mean to see Maggie for myself. I want to come in.' I pushed at the door, but she held it fast, and I knew that I was no match for her in terms of physical strength. She stood nearly a head taller than I, and was sturdily built.

'I'm afraid you can't,' she said. 'Go

away. You have Maggie's message and her apologies. I think that will be sufficient.'

'I think not. And if you do not let me in, right now, I will go directly from here to the police. I think you will let them in.'

Her eyes narrowed and for a moment she regarded me with chilling malice. Then, having made her decision, she stepped suddenly aside.

'Very well,' she said, motioning for me to enter.

I stepped into the hall. The door closed behind me. The house was dark. Outside it was twilight, and within none of the lights were on yet. It was as if I had stepped into a tomb.

18

As the door closed behind me, I braced myself inwardly. I dared not let Elisa know that I was frightened.

'I'll tell Maggie you're here,' she said, starting around me toward the stairs, 'and see if she wants to see you, although I warn you she said she did not wish to be disturbed.'

I did not intend to be put off that easily.

'Never mind,' I said, moving faster than she did. 'I'll tell her myself.' Before she could stop me I was hurrying up the stairs. She followed close behind.

There was the slight possibility that Maggie really did not want to be disturbed, and reminding myself of this I paused at her closed door and knocked. There was no reply. Elisa joined me there.

'See for yourself,' she said, opening the bedroom door. 'Maggie is sound asleep. She's been quite exhausted the last several days. That was why she decided against taking a trip; she just did not feel up to it right now.'

The room was dark. The drapes were closed and the light from the hall was just enough to let me make out the small figure curled up on the bed.

'Maggie?' I called softly.

There was no reply. 'You see?' Elisa said, moving to close the door.

'No, I don't,' I said. I blocked her move and stepped into the bedroom, calling 'Maggie' again, louder this time. Again there was no reply.

I went to the bed and put a hand on one of the thin shoulders, shaking it gently, and repeated her name once more. There was still no response. She might have been dead. That thought sent a chill through me.

I found the switch to the light beside the bed and turned it on, blinking my eyes against the sudden brightness. I leaned close to the bed, putting my ear against Maggie's breast. She was breathing. I had little enough training in nursing; whether her breathing was fast or slow or just normal, I could not tell. It looked as though she were only in a normal sleep, but I knew that normal sleep was not so sound as this. I shook her again, with no more success than before.

'Something's wrong with her,' I said to Elisa as I straightened up from the bed. 'She won't wake up.'

Elisa shrugged as though this were of no consequence. 'I told you she's been quite exhausted,' she said.

That explanation was far from satisfactory with me. 'Or perhaps she has been drugged,' I suggested, looking down at Maggie again.

'She has rather strong sleeping pills,' Elisa said. 'Perhaps she's taken some of those, in which case I'm not surprised that she's a little hard to wake up.'

'She's more than a little hard to wake up, as you put it,' I said caustically. I was certain Maggie was indeed drugged, and not by her own hand either. But what on earth did one do about it? How did one counteract the influence of drugs, especially without knowing what Elisa had given her? I thought I remembered that cold water on the wrists helped to waken sleeping persons, and surely some strong coffee, if I could get her awake enough to drink it without choking.

I went to the cord that summoned Miss Wright and tugged at it, ignoring Elisa's unwavering stare. I waited several minutes, but Miss Wright did not appear. I knew that she was usually quite prompt in answering Maggie's summons, and I gave another tug at the rope.

'Miss Wright is gone,' Elisa said from across the room.

'Gone?' I turned to look at her disbelievingly. For all Miss Wright's blandness, she had seemed content here; I could not imagine that she would just disappear into the night on such short notice. 'What do you mean, gone? This isn't her night off.'

'Maggie dismissed her.'

'I don't believe it,' I said curtly. 'Maggie was perfectly happy with Miss Wright. Why would she dismiss her so suddenly, for no apparent reason?'

Elisa shrugged again; my disbelief seemed to matter little to her. 'Perhaps she dismissed her because she was planning to take a trip. Perhaps she found Miss Wright stealing something from the house. I'm sure I don't know, and care little. All I do know is that Miss Wright is no longer in the house nor in Maggie's employ. And it's just as well, actually. I can manage to take care of Maggie quite well, for the time being.'

In this context, that phrase had an ominous ring. 'What do you mean, for the time being?' I asked.

She smiled one of her icy smiles at me; it made my blood run cold. 'You know what I mean,' she replied. 'It's become blatantly apparent that Maggie is no longer in possession of her faculties. The best thing will be to have her put someplace where there are professional people to look after her and see that she does no harm to herself or to anyone else. I've already begun the arrangements.'

'Ken will never agree to that, and you know it,' I said, recognizing as I said it the futility of my argument. Elisa had no doubt gone through all of this very carefully.

'His permission won't be necessary,' she said. 'As a matter of fact, he's been dismissed also. He's no longer Maggie's physician.'

'That's not true,' I said. 'I spoke to him just today. He's still looking after Maggie.'

'He'll be informed in the morning that his services are no longer required. I've engaged another doctor who's already examined Maggie and confirmed my worst suspicions.'

'And no doubt he's another of your stooges,' I said. 'Has he examined Maggie in that condition?' I pointed at the inert figure on the bed. 'Or is he the one who put her in that state?'

'Maggie's health is her doctor's concern.'

'Well I'm not buying that,' I said. 'I demand that another doctor examine Maggie, at once. I want someone here to look her over. Or I want her taken to a hospital. She's more than just asleep, and this is more than the result of sleeping pills.'

'My instructions were that she was not to be disturbed, so she certainly will not go to any hospital. As for an examination by a doctor, as I told you, she's already had one, and I think that should suffice.'

'Then I want to meet this doctor of hers,' I insisted. 'I want to talk to him. I want to determine for myself if he knows of this . . . this coma she's in. I want to know to what he attributes it, and what, if anything, should be done about it.'

'He's quite aware of how she's sleeping. She was like this when he examined her.'

'Oh?' My eyebrows went up. 'And in this condition he was able to determine that Maggie is not sane?'

She saw her mistake, and for a change her icy poise faltered. 'Why . . . he examined her twice,' she stammered. 'He examined her earlier, when she was conscious. And he gave her a sedative to put her to sleep. He said she'd had too many things and too many people exciting her needlessly. He said he thought you should be kept away from her.'

'I'm sure he did.' I did not try to keep the sarcasm from my voice. 'Nonetheless, I don't intend to just ignore this. If you won't call your doctor whoever-he-is, then I will call Doctor Wolfe.'

'You have no authority in this,' she warned me.

'On the contrary, I have as much or more authority here than you do. Maggie is my aunt. If necessary, I can call my mother and have her here in a few hours. She's Maggie's sister and I think any court would recognize her authority in this matter.'

I had gone to the nightstand and lifted the telephone receiver before I remembered that the instrument was disconnected. I replaced it on its cradle. Elisa was smiling in that frightening way of hers. I had forgotten in my anger that with Maggie unconscious and Miss Wright gone, I was quite alone in this house with Elisa and, presumably, her friend Davis.

'I'm going,' I said, managing to sound quite calm despite my inner feelings of fear. 'But I must warn you that I will be back with Doctor Wolfe. I would suggest that you have your doctor friend here to justify his opinion. Doctor Wolfe has something of a temper.'

She moved as though to follow me, but I added quickly, 'Don't bother to show me out,' and left the room as swiftly as I could without seeming to flee from her. To my relief, she did not follow me at once or try to keep me from leaving. I had feared my threats might bring her to try to prevent my getting in touch with Ken.

She was still upstairs when I reached the first floor. It was this fact that tempted me to investigate. As I came by the door of the library, I chanced to glance inside that room. My eyes fell immediately on a tape recorder sitting on one of the tables.

I stopped short, staring at the instrument. There was a tape already on it. I was thinking of the movies I had watched with Sam Carr, the Buddy Berke movies, and my own hunch that Elisa and Davis had made a tape from the old soundtracks, a tape to convince Maggie that her dead son was giving her messages from the spirit world. If I had those tapes, I would have no difficulty in convincing Maggie of the truth of my theory.

I glanced toward the stairs. Elisa was

still nowhere in sight. It would take only a moment to confirm my suspicions. I stepped into the library and hurried to the tape recorder.

I was not particularly familiar with this sort of equipment, but the controls were marked and not complicated. The flip of a switch, a twirl of a dial, and it was on, the tape rushing through the playing heads.

At first there was nothing but a humming sound, and I thought that I must have been mistaken. Then, just as I was about to turn the machine off, I heard the now-familiar voice of Maggie's dead son.

'Mother, Mother,' he cried. 'How could you?' This was followed by plaintive sobbing.

It sent a chill racing up my spine. It was eerie to hear this cry put together from his old movies. It sounded so real that I could well understand Maggie's being fooled by it. I almost answered him myself.

There was more on the tape, with long pauses between the various pieces of dialogue. 'She has to go,' he said simply. I knew who that had been meant to refer to. Small wonder that Maggie had been in such a dither about letting me stay once I had arrived.

With me moved out of the house and Miss Wright gone, Elisa and Davis had apparently grown careless. They had assumed there was no further need to hide this equipment. Probably they had finished with it; it had served its purpose in getting rid of me and driving Maggie to the verge of insanity. But the tape was just the valuable evidence I needed to combat them. I toyed with the dials until I managed to reverse the tape. It seemed to rewind with agonizing slowness, but finally it was back to the beginning.

I snatched the tape-reel from the machine with a sense of triumph and whirled about to leave.

My triumph was short-lived. Davis stood just inside the door, blocking my escape.

19

'Excuse me,' I said, trying to make the reel of tape I held as inconspicuous as possible at my side. 'I was just leaving.'

I tried to move around him, but with no success. He completely blocked the exit.

'Please let me by,' I insisted.

'With that tape?' he asked. He made a grab for me. I tried to keep the tape away from him, but it was useless. He seized me in his powerful grip and yanked the reel out of my hand.

'Let me go,' I cried, struggling helplessly against him. Elisa appeared behind him.

'What's going on?' she demanded.

'She knows,' Davis said, brandishing the tape. 'I heard her playing this.'

I knew there was no point in trying to lie about it; he had the evidence in his hand. The only thing I could try to do was bluff my way out of this predicament.

'Yes, you're right,' I said brazenly. 'I did listen to that tape, and I know how and why you used it. And I intend to go to the authorities about it, whether you keep the tape or not. So I'd suggest that you let me go before you make things even worse for yourself.'

'Shut up,' Davis said. He gave me a violent shove, and I stumbled and fell back, landing hard on the floor. I thought for a moment he was going to beat me, but he turned to Elisa instead. 'We can't let her go now,' he said. 'She knows too much.'

Elisa's cold gaze settled on me once again. I knew I could expect no pity from her. 'You're right,' she said. 'But the question is, what do we do with her? We can't send her to the asylum too, and we can't just keep her here. That boyfriend of hers would be around looking for her sooner or later.'

'We'll have to kill her,' Davis said.

He said it with such an even tone that my heart nearly stopped beating. This was no idle threat intended to frighten me into submission. This was a simple statement of fact he believed in.

'Don't be foolish,' I said, speaking rapidly. 'Everyone would know who was responsible from the moment they found out.'

'Would they?' Elisa asked. 'You're forgetting, everyone knows that Maggie's voices instructed her to kill you. That's why you were moved out of here. Your boyfriend even knows that. But if you were foolish enough to come back alone and Maggie, out of her mind, killed you . . . why, what could be done to us? I tried several times to persuade you to stay away. And Davis is only the maintenance man.'

I could think of nothing to say in answer. I stared at her in horror, realizing the truth of what she said. If anything happened to me, it would be easy for them to pin it on poor crazy Maggie. Perhaps with hypnosis they could even persuade her to confess.

'The question is, how do we do it?' Davis asked.

'I don't know.' Elisa was thoughtful for a moment. 'Maybe we could kill two birds with one stone, so to speak. A murder-suicide scheme. Like burning the house down. It would look like Maggie killed her and then killed herself in the fire.'

'Only we lose the house,' Davis said.

It was like a macabre game of some sort, sitting listening to these two plot how I was going to die. My eyes darted about, looking for some way of escape, even some weapon with which to defend myself. There was nothing. I was trapped here, at their mercy, with nothing but my wits to save me.

'It won't work,' I said aloud, taking a desperate tack. 'Ken is on his way here. He'll be here in a few minutes.'

For a moment Elisa looked alarmed. Then the crafty smile settled on her lips again. 'No he isn't,' she said. 'If he was, you wouldn't have been leaving to go get him.'

Her reply gave me one slim hope. Ken might come in time, if I could stall long enough. It was only a slight chance, but it was all I had to go on just now.

'You've been so clever,' I said to her. While I spoke, I got up from the floor, careful to make no sudden moves that would bring a response from Davis. I seated myself in a chair. 'You have such a brilliant scheme to get what you wanted.'

She accepted the flattery as her apparent due, but I knew she had been around Maggie long enough to have absorbed some of her appetite for compliments. 'Yes, it was clever of me, wasn't it?' she agreed.

'I'll bet you were perturbed when I came into the picture, weren't you?' I said.

'Very. I had hoped that the falling chandelier would send you flying back home. But when it didn't, we had to resort to other means.'

'Maggie's warnings?' I asked. 'And her spirit voices?'

'Yes. We did those while she slept. It's a form of hypnosis. A few of those sessions and she was ripe to believe anything we did.'

'Including those phony séances with Madame Divina. I suppose she was just doing it for pay?'

Elisa nodded. 'Very generous pay. She

was also the ghost who haunted your room. I knew you'd suspect me and come straight to my room; that's why we used her.'

'I really didn't think of her,' I admitted. 'And the tapes — made from the movie soundtracks, right?'

'Right. That was Davis's idea.'

'And Maggie's visit to the cemetery?'

'More hypnosis,' she said. 'I dressed her. All we had to do was get her to move around a little, and to forget everything when she woke up.'

I shook my head sadly. 'And to think, you did all of this just to get this house, which you already live in, and Maggie's money, which she already shares with you.'

Elisa threw back her head and laughed, but there was nothing pleasant or uplifting about that sound. 'You fool,' she said to me when the laughter had passed. 'Do you think I did it so I could inherit the house?'

'That's the way I heard it,' Davis said, looking surprised.

'Oh, I'll admit,' she said to him, 'after

you came, that was a part of it. Maggie would never have gone along with your moving right into the house, or marrying me. We'd have had to go out on our own. But that wasn't the real reason, not to begin with.'

'Then why . . . ?' I asked.

'Because I hated her,' she said with such vehemence that I was shocked into silence. 'Do you know what it's like to live in the same house with Maggie Berke, the fabulous Maggie Berke, and her precious multi-million-dollar son? When you yourself are ugly and poor, an unwanted stepchild of a father who just happened to be one of La Berke's husbands before he died? No, you don't know. How could you? Look at you. Young, beautiful, well-to-do, talented. How could you understand what it was like to be me?'

'But she took you in,' I said.

'A charity case,' she said scornfully. 'I wasn't even that. I was a housemaid, a nursemaid to that brat, a hired hand, a professional companion. Good old dumpy reliable Elisa.'

'But surely she must have shared some of her life with you,' I said, unable to

218

believe that Maggie had been knowingly cruel. 'Parties, social functions. The house was full of them in those days.'

'Oh yes. And if I minded my Ps and Qs, I was allowed to mingle.' She looked away from me, a dreamy look coming over her face, and I realized that she was reliving that long-ago past. 'Once, there was a young man. Oh, he was handsome and charming. Not the sort you'd imagine with me at all. I met him here, at one of those parties of Maggie's. He paid court to me, and I fell head-over-heels in love with him. Then one night he asked me if I would talk to Maggie about getting him a part in a particular movie. I realized he'd been courting me to get favors out of Maggie.'

'But that wasn't Maggie's fault,' I said, but she did not even hear me.

'Then there was that other night. For a year I had been looking forward to a premiere. It was very special. I got that young man the part, you see, on the promise that I would be his date for that night, and we would announce our engagement. Of course, I had to keep that secret from Maggie. But when that evening came, the little brat was sick — a bad cold, the flu I guess. Someone had to stay with him. Maggie asked me if I would. I finally explained why I couldn't; that I was to meet Terry — that was his name. She was surprised and sorry for me. What I didn't know, but she did, was that he wouldn't be there. He had left that morning to begin shooting another picture. He hadn't even let me know.'

She paused, and her face showed still the anguish she had felt on that occasion. 'So I stayed home with Buddy. And I hated him even more than I had before — that spoiled, pretty, rich little kid. So when he wouldn't stop crying, I gave him some of my sleeping pills to knock him out. And then, while I was staring at him, thinking of all my instructions to keep him covered up and keep him warm and do this and don't do that, I thought, 'What am I killing myself for, to keep him alive? If he were dead, Maggie would have to love me, care about me, pay attention to me. I would be all she had.'

'So I took off all the covers, and his

pajamas, and I carried him into the bathroom, and put him in a tub of icy water; and I opened all of the windows, so that the cold night air was blowing across him. And I left him there and went downstairs to read a book.'

I gasped in horror. 'Elisa — you . . . you killed him!'

'Yes. I left him there all night. And when it was nearly dawn, and I knew Maggie would soon be coming home, I went up and put him back in bed and dried him off. He was burning up with a fever; it was sky-high. When Maggie came in I cried a lot and said how I had tried to find her at all the different parties, and how he had cried for her. Oh, she tried to get him to a hospital, but it was too late. The exposure on top of the flu he already had was too much for him.'

I buried my face in my hands, sickened by the grisly tale. I could scarcely believe anyone could be driven to such cruelty.

'Only it didn't work,' she said bitterly. 'Because when he was dead and buried, I was still just plain, dumpy old Elisa, and I was still stuck in this house with her. All she did then was sit around and moan about how she had killed him. The first thing in my life I did on my own and I couldn't even take credit for it.' She narrowed her eyes malevolently. 'And I came to hate her. Oh, how I hated her. I wanted to make her suffer the way I had suffered. I began to haunt her. I began to encourage her guilt. I wanted to drive her mad.'

She was breathless with excitement. Suddenly she straightened her shoulders. She seemed to have regained her senses as quickly as she had lost them. 'Then Davis came. And we decided that if we could get her put away, we could have the house and the money and be rid of her. That's when we really started on her.'

'Well, it was the house and the money I wanted,' Davis said. 'I don't care about any of the rest of it. Only, we got to do something with her.' He jerked a thumb in my direction.

I hadn't managed to stall more than a few minutes, and I knew that even if Ken came it would not be for a long time yet.

'Tell me . . . ' I began.

'I've told you enough,' Elisa said, as if she had read my thoughts. 'Bring her upstairs.'

I tried to struggle against Davis but I was no match for his brute strength. I was half led, half carried up the stairs to my old room.

'You'll keep fine in here,' Elisa said as Davis shoved me inside, 'while we decide what to do with you.'

The door slammed after them. I heard the key turn in the lock and then a grating sound as it was removed.

20

I leaned my cheek against the solid wood of the door. I could hear their muffled voices as they moved away down the hall, talking to one another. I did not need to ponder the subject under discussion.

I waited until long after they had gone, lest they change their minds for some reason and start back. When I was certain they had gone downstairs, I left the door and went across the room to the nightstand beside my bed. There, in a drawer, beneath a neat stack of handkerchiefs, was the key I had thought to obtain earlier. I had found myself locked in this room once before, shortly after my arrival. I had promised myself that the next time I would be prepared. This was the next time, and I was indeed prepared.

I knew that the key worked; I had tried it before. I had not given any attention, however, to the rusty condition of both the lock and the key. They made a squeaking sound that seemed to my anxious ears to be a shrieking alarm. I leaned against the door, holding my breath and listening in fear.

There was no sound of an approach, and after a long moment of agonized waiting, I opened the door and crept into the hall.

The door to Maggie's room was unlocked. She was still unconscious. I knelt beside the bed, my lips close to her ear, and repeated her name.

'Maggie,' I begged, glancing over my shoulder at the open door. 'Wake up. Please, Maggie, wake up.' She stirred ever so faintly and a low moan escaped her lips, but she did not awaken. In desperation I slapped her cheeks with the palm of my hand. Not even this roused her from her drugged stupor.

I tried lifting her from the bed. However, small and frail as she was, I knew I could not manage to carry her down the stairs, out of the house, and to safety.

I stood, looking anxiously around the room for some solution to my dilemma. I went to the window and looked down. If I could make some sort of sling for her, perhaps I could lower her to the ground. But the risks of that approach were readily apparent. Even if I managed to get her to the ground without dropping her, which I was not at all sure of, I still had the task of escaping with her.

A shadow crossed the square of light from the window below. The library was directly below Maggie's room, and Elisa and Davis were in that room. Obviously I could not even try to lower Maggie past that window without attracting their attention.

I came back to the bed, walking as though on eggs. I dared not let them hear a sound that would bring them to investigate.

As much as I regretted it, there was only one thing that I could do. I had to escape alone, to someplace where I could call Ken, or the police, and get help for Maggie. On my own I stood a good chance of getting away; taking Maggie with me in her unconscious state was only inviting disaster.

'I'll be back,' I promised her in a whisper.

I stole again into the hall. It stretched before me ominously, a no-man's-land that I had to traverse if I wanted to escape. The lights were on. To turn them off would attract attention. I had to walk the entire length of the corridor, make my way down the stairs, and somehow get past the library.

The corridor seemed miles long. I moved quickly, staying close to the wall, aware that each second was precious. My ears strained to make out the sound of their voices below; that would tell me they were still engaged in their conversation in the library.

Not until I was on the stairs, moving cautiously downward, could I distinguish the sounds enough to be confident they were still there. They were arguing, judging from the inflections of their voices.

The door to the library was closed. As I neared the last step, I braced myself for a wild dash to the front door. I let go my hold on the banister and tensed to run. Then, suddenly, Davis's voice grew louder. He was coming to the door! I looked frantically about, but there was no place for me to hide. Heart in throat, I pressed back against the wall.

'All this arguing ain't getting us anywhere,' he said, flinging open the door to the hall. His shadow fell menacingly across the hall, seeming a wall that cut me off from the door and escape. 'I'm gonna go up and bring her down here. You leave her to me.'

The wall felt cold against the palms of my hands and I realized that I was sweating. In my imagination I almost thought I smelled the danger about to face me.

'Wait,' Elisa said as he started through the door. He paused and turned back.

If I tried to go down the hall, to the safety of the open door to the dining room, I risked detection. But if I remained where I was, detection was certain. Not even daring to breathe, I moved away from the wall, took the last step, and began to edge my way around the stairwell.

'I don't want anything to go wrong at this stage,' Elisa said. 'There's no telling how much she's told that doctor friend of hers, and he's bound to be suspicious of whatever happens. We've got to make it look right.'

'You just leave it to me,' he said.

I was around the newel post . . . across the hall . . . and finally, trembling with terror, through the doorway, into the dining room.

'Be right back,' he said, his voice moving up the stairs. 'You get me a fresh beer.'

I could not escape down the hall, not with the library door open. But I had remembered the back door, out of the kitchen.

I had reached the kitchen, closing the swinging door after myself gently so that it would make no noise, when the significance of Davis's last remark hit me. Elisa would be coming to the kitchen for the beer he had requested.

At almost the same instant, I heard Elisa's heavy footsteps crossing the dining room. There was no time to reach the door, unbolt it, and get through it. There was not even time to hide. I stepped back behind the swing of the door, flattening myself hard against the broom cabinet behind me, as the door pushed open. It swung against me. I prayed that she would not push it hard, hard enough to discover the obstacle behind it that prevented its opening completely. She didn't. The door rested against me, partially shielding me from view. But only partially. If she looked around . . .

I heard the refrigerator door open and close. A drawer slid open. The bottle made a wooshing sound as she removed its cap. I held my breath, certain that she must hear the roaring in my ears. My lungs threatened to burst; my heart beat a violent rhythm.

Davis's footsteps clattered above. 'She's gone!' he yelled as he came noisily down the stairs.

The beer fell from Elisa's hand as she whirled about, already running for the door. I saw a stream of the pale yellow liquid race across the floor, looking like an accusing finger that, had she followed its direction, would have pointed directly to me.

His announcement had saved me from discovery. In her shock she ran by without even looking in my direction. As she went through the doorway, I gave the swinging door a gentle shove. It swung shut in her wake, as though she might have tugged it. I prayed that she would not notice it in her excitement.

'The front door's still locked,' I heard her call to him. 'She must still be in the house.'

'The back way . . . ?' he yelled.

'I was just there,' she said. 'She didn't go out that way.'

I raced to the door, flinging back the heavy old bolt, and threw the door open. At the most I had only seconds to spare. The night air was a heady perfume that made me almost intoxicated. I was free, out of the house, out of their grip.

I ran like I had never run before — through the garden, around the corner of the house, along the terrace. I was almost to the front of the house when I heard the front door thrown open.

'If she's got away . . . ' Davis said.

I flattened myself against the wall as the

outside lights came on, blinding me with their brilliance.

Elisa's voice came from the other direction, from behind me. 'Davis,' she cried, 'the back door's open. She got out this way. She's outside.'

I threw myself down, ignoring the pain that shot through my skinned knee; a sprawling yucca plant hid me from view. Davis came running around the corner, headed for the rear.

'She's in the garden,' he called to Elisa. 'That's where she'd try to hide.'

I didn't even wait for him to pass out of sight. As soon as he had gone past me, I jumped up, slipping my feet from my shoes, and began to run again. I reached the corner of the house. Then I was around it, fleeing wildly across the front lawn. And at last I was on the drive, its hard surface letting me go faster.

Not fast enough, however. I heard a shout behind me, and I knew I was discovered. 'There she goes!' Davis called. 'Come on, catch her!'

'No, wait,' Elisa answered. 'The car.'

I looked back to see them racing for the

garage. Elisa reached it first, sliding behind the wheel of the big sedan parked there. The engine roared to life and by the time Davis had reached the car it was already gliding from the garage, down the drive.

I must reach the street, I thought desperately. *Surely once I've reached there, where people can see, they wouldn't dare run me down.*

Even as I thought this, though, I knew it was futile. I was at the end of my strength. My chest hurt with the agony of my exertion, and every breath sent shockwaves of pain crashing through my lungs. My feet felt as though they were made of lead.

The headlights swept over me. The engine roared louder as the car surged forward, sweeping toward the first bend. I looked back again. The yards of distance that it had taken me minutes to run would take them only seconds. The car came about the first wide curve with its tires squealing in protest.

I was still far from the street. I knew without calculating speed and distance, that I could not reach it in time. There was no other route open. To the left a rock wall dropped the equivalent of three stories, to the Sunset Strip. I could not go down that way. To my right, beyond a patch of trees, was the high wall that surrounded the property.

I summoned up the last of my strength for a final burst of speed, desperately seeking to gain the wall. My foot turned at an inept angle, and I was suddenly tumbling to the ground, scraping shins and elbows and hands on the concrete. I tried to scramble to my feet again, but a shockwave of pain shot upward from my ankle. I had turned it in the fall.

I turned horrified eyes on the car bearing down upon me. I was directly in their path. The engine roared louder as Elisa accelerated. There was no way I could escape.

In that awful moment as I lay in the path of that onrushing motor car, I surrendered to the idea that I would die. It seemed so inevitable that even hope fled, leaving me abandoned.

What happened next occurred so

swiftly and so unexpectedly that I had no sense of its reality. It was rather like a fragment of a dream that lingers in the mind when one has awakened, realistic but not real.

I saw a movement in the brush near me, and then a young boy stepped from the growth of trees and bushes that bordered the wall. He came toward me, running, his hands outstretched; I thought he had seen me fall and was coming to help me to my feet. In the same moment, I realized that he had not yet noticed the car racing toward us.

'Go back!' I screamed.

He halted suddenly, seeing the oncoming headlights for the first time. But he was already in their path.

'Go back!' I cried again. He had stopped still, and stared at the car now as if not believing what he saw.

There was a sudden screeching as Elisa slammed on the brakes. I heard her scream. The car veered and slid almost out of control. She was so close that I could see the look of horror on her face; could watch as she gave the steering wheel a violent yank. The car careened to the left, toward the drop to the Strip. There was a ripping of metal and a duet of screams from within as the car shot through the railing and plunged over the wall. I heard the crash below.

I lay stunned, hardly believing what I had seen. What had caused Elisa's moment of panic; what had sent her plummeting over the cliff? Had some forgotten conscience caught up with her, denying her the privilege of killing an innocent youngster as well as me?

At that thought I remembered for the first time since the crash my mysterious benefactor, the errant trespasser who had, in making his childish exploration of the grounds, managed to save my life. I turned to thank him but he was gone. I was alone on the drive.

'Hello,' I called aloud, looking all around. 'Come back. Don't be frightened, please. I want to thank you.'

But there was no sign of him. I tried to stand, but my ankle still refused to support me. There was nothing I could do but lie where I was and wait to be discovered; and while I waited, I thought of the young man who had gone as quickly as he had come. No doubt the crash had frightened him. I determined that I would find him. If necessary I would place huge ads, or rent a billboard. I owed him, after all, my life.

As it turned out, I did not have long to wait to be discovered. Within a few minutes headlights turned in at the gates. I sat up so that I would be seen and waved my arms. There was a squeal of brakes; a door crashed open. I had a glimpse of a beloved figure racing toward me, and then I was in Ken's wonderful arms.

What followed of course was a whirlwind of confusion. Elisa and Davis had crashed to the street below almost directly in Ken's path. Davis had died almost at once. Elisa was by this time on her way to a hospital, in critical condition.

There was Maggie to look after, of course, and my ankle to be tended. Ken called an ambulance for Maggie, and then bandaged my foot.

'I'd rather wait here,' I told him when he suggested I might want to go to the hospital as well. 'If you'll bring me one of those old canes in Maggie's closet, I'll get around all right on this.'

'I'll be back as soon as I can,' he said when the ambulance attendants had carried Maggie out on a stretcher. He kissed me lightly.

'I'll be here,' I assured him.

It was nearly morning, however, when he finally returned. A weak but ambulatory Maggie was with him, entering the house on his arm. She embraced me warmly.

'I know how much I have to thank you for,' she said tearfully. 'My dear, how you have suffered, and for my sake. But I shall repay you, I promise.'

'You already have,' I told her. 'In a thousand different ways.' After a moment, I remembered and asked, 'Elisa?'

Maggie bowed her head sadly. 'She died soon after I arrived at the hospital,' Ken said. 'She was hysterical at the end.'

'Hysterical?' Maggie said. 'I don't think so, if you'll pardon my disagreeing with you, Doctor.'

'I don't understand,' I said, looking

from one to the other.

'Elisa thought she saw Buddy,' Ken explained. 'She said his ghost made her wreck the car.'

I stared in bewilderment. 'Why, there was a boy,' I said. 'But it was just some young man from the neighborhood. He saw me fall and came out from the trees to help me up. Elisa saw him and swerved to try to keep from hitting him. That's how she went over the edge.'

'Elisa says it was Buddy,' Maggie said softly but firmly. 'She says she saw him clearly. He was directly in her headlights. It terrified her so, that she lost her head and lost control of the car.'

There was one of the many portraits of Buddy on the wall behind Maggie. I stared at it thoughtfully. Elisa had been hysterical of course, as Ken said, and an unknown boy had appeared to her to be the young man whose death she had caused in the past. But it was easy to see how she had made that mistake. Remembering the young man who had saved me and looking now at the portrait, I could see that there was more than a passing similarity between the two faces. Of course, it had been dark when I had seen the boy. Still, it gave one an eerie feeling.

'She was just hysterical,' Ken said again, putting an arm about my shoulders.

Maggie shook her head stubbornly. 'No, I don't choose to believe that,' she said. 'All these years since Buddy's death, I've suffered guilt that no one else could ever understand. I believed, from what Elisa told me, that he blamed me for his death, and with some justification. This guilt has poisoned my every thought, my every deed. Perhaps I have been as insane as Elisa tried to make me out to be. Certainly I have been foolish.'

'But understandably so,' I said.

She smiled gratefully. 'Thank you, but I need no excuses for my foolishness. That's in the past now, you see. That foolishness is over for me. Because I believe Buddy did come back. Not in all those séances and visitations that I believed in before; Ken has already told me how phony they were, and I realize now that I was duped because I wanted to be duped. But I believe Buddy came back tonight, not only to save Mari and me, but to show me that he had forgiven me; that I need suffer no longer.'

There was a moment's silence. 'Well, as a man of science, I'm not certain I can accept that theory,' Ken said. 'But science is not always right, as you know.'

I looked again at the portrait. Maggie's statement had touched me, and in that fleeting instant it almost seemed to me as if that painted face smiled down upon us. 'There are more things than we can hope to understand,' I said, glad for the solid feel of Ken's arm about me.

★   ★   ★

I came to The Aerie a year afterward. It was greatly changed by this time. Maggie no longer lived in the house. With the lifting of that awful weight from her shoulders, she had seemed to shed years. She had come from her semi-retirement to enter once again into a life of glamor and varied activities. Once again her face, seeming hardly less lovely than it had been twenty years before, graced magazine covers. Her name was in virtually every column, more than once in a romantic context. And she was rehearsing for her stage debut in an exciting new play written especially for her. She was, in short, very much the star again, perhaps even bigger than before.

As for The Aerie, she had turned that massive house into a museum devoted to the history of the cinematic arts. Many of her own mementoes she had left behind, and a generous trust fund had assured the place of longevity. Other stars, especially those from the lustrous past of the cinema, had made their own splendid contributions. Old movies were shown daily in the small theater that had been built on the grounds. Best of all, everything was free to young people, 'in memory of Buddy,' Maggie explained when she took me on a guided tour of the newly opened Buddy Berke Movie Museum.

I found myself thinking, as I strolled from room to room, that the shadows were gone now. The gloom and tragedy that had truly haunted this house had departed as surely as had the spirit of Buddy.

'I wish you would stay for a time,'

Maggie said when the tour was over. 'There's so much happening just now. I have a divine party to attend tonight, and I know you would be a smash success there. And dinner at Chasens. They've been begging me to make an appearance. And tomorrow we could drive up to Malibu. I've met the most heavenly artist there. He says he wants to sculpt my face, but I've been putting him off.'

'I wish I could,' I said, smiling at her new enthusiasm. 'But I have an impatient husband at home who might take a dim view of my being the smash of a cocktail party.'

Things had changed a great deal for me, too. I was Mrs. Ken Wolfe now. And for all Maggie's flattery, I could not really imagine that an about-to-be mother would be the smash of any cocktail party.

THE END

We do hope that you have enjoyed reading this large print book.

Did you know that all of our titles are available for purchase?

We publish a wide range of high quality large print books including:
Romances, Mysteries, Classics
General Fiction
Non Fiction and Westerns

Special interest titles available in large print are:
The Little Oxford Dictionary
Music Book, Song Book
Hymn Book, Service Book

Also available from us courtesy of Oxford University Press:
Young Readers' Dictionary
(large print edition)
Young Readers' Thesaurus
(large print edition)

For further information or a free brochure, please contact us at:
Ulverscroft Large Print Books Ltd.,
The Green, Bradgate Road, Anstey,
Leicester, LE7 7FU, England.
Tel: (00 44) **0116 236 4325**
Fax: (00 44) **0116 234 0205**

Other titles in the
Linford Mystery Library:

STORM EVIL

John Robb

A terrible storm sweeps across a vast desert of North Africa. Five legionnaires and a captain on a training course are caught in it and take refuge in a ruined temple. Into the temple, too, come four Arabs laden with hate for the Legion captain. Then a beautiful aviator arrives — the estranged wife of the officer. When darkness falls, and the storm rages outside, the Arabs take a slow and terrible vengeance against the captain. Death strikes suddenly, often, and in a grotesque form . . .

ROOKIE COP

Richard A. Lupoff

America, June 1940. Nick Train has given up his dreams of a boxing championship after a brief and unsuccessful career in the ring. When one of his pals takes the examination for the police academy, Nick decides to join him. But what started out as a whim turns into a dangerous challenge, as Nick plays a precarious double game of collector for the mob and mole for a shadowy enforcement body . . . Will the rookie cop's luck hold?

THE DEVIL'S DANCE

V. J. Banis

When Chris leaves New York for a vacation with her half-sister Pam, who is staying at a Tennessee country mansion, she discovers that the remote backwater is the site of a centuries-old feud raging between the Andrewses and the Melungeons; and Chris's elderly host, Mrs. Andrews, lives in fear. Danger lurks everywhere, from the deceptively tranquil countryside to the darkly handsome, yet mysterious, Gabe who hides amid the shadows. And when events take a more sinister turn, it seems that the curse of the Melungeons is hungry for more victims . . .

FIND THE LADY

Norman Firth

When gangster Mike Spagliotti is found shot through the head inside his locked New York hotel suite, it is a perplexing problem for Detective-Inspector Flannel. And when newspaper reporter Anita Curzon begins to interfere, Flannel's temper does not improve . . . In *The Egyptian Tomb* Tony Gilmour and his friends Ron and Alan travel to Egypt to investigate the suspicious death of Ron's father — but they are dogged by enemies who will stop at nothing to ensure that no one discovers the secret of the tomb of Ko Len Tep!

MIDNIGHT RAIN

Arlette Lees

In the dark days of the Great Depression, Detective Jack Dunning and his partner Jim Tunney are investigating the deaths of two young boys found on the same stretch of highway in recent weeks. Could their deaths be connected to the disappearance of three girls from the Saguaro Correctional Institution in the isolated Mojave Desert? How does the mysterious Deutschlander Social Club fit into the picture? And Jack's beautiful live-in girlfriend, Angel Doll, has problems of her own when a threatening figure emerges from her troubled past . . .

THE HANGMAN

Gerald Verner

Death stalks through the residential district of Hill Green, carrying off two prominent members of the community in two days. The first is a man found hanging from a lamp-post; the second, a young woman found hanging from a beam in the roof of a barn. When found, both corpses have a small card pinned to their clothing, bearing the same pencilled message: WITH THE COMPLIMENTS OF THE HANGMAN. Detective-Inspector Shadgold of Scotland Yard soon realises this is going to be one of his toughest cases . . .